# Looking for Love

**National Association for Visually Handicapped**
------------------------- *serving the partially seeing*

As the Founder/CEO of NAVH, the only national health agency solely devoted to those who, although not totally blind, have an eye disease which could lead to serious visual impairment, I am pleased to recognize Thorndike Press* as one of the leading publishers in the large print field.

Founded in 1954 in San Francisco to prepare large print textbooks for partially seeing children, NAVH became the pioneer and standard setting agency in the preparation of large type.

Today, those publishers who meet our standards carry the prestigious "Seal of Approval" indicating high quality large print. We are delighted that Thorndike Press is one of the publishers whose titles meet these standards. We are also pleased to recognize the significant contribution Thorndike Press is making in this important and growing field.

Lorraine H. Marchi, L.H.D.
Founder/CEO
NAVH

* Thorndike Press encompasses the following imprints: Thorndike, Wheeler, Walker and Large Print Press.

# *Looking for Love*

*Also by Barbara Cartland*
*in Large Print:*

The Call of the Highlands
A Coronation of Love
Love Strikes a Devil
Revenge of the Heart
Terror from the Throne
Bride to the King
A Caretaker of Love
A Duke in Danger
From Hate to Love
A Kiss in Rome
Lights, Laughter and a Lady
Love Climbs In
The Love Puzzle
A Night of Gaiety
Ola and the Sea Wolf
The Prude and the Prodigal
Secret Harbour

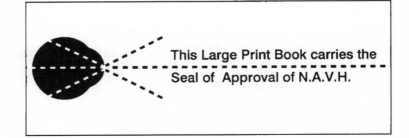

# Looking for Love

## Barbara Cartland

WHEELER PUBLISHING

Copyright © 1982 by Barbara Cartland.

All rights reserved.

Published in 2004 by arrangement with International Book
Marketing Limited.

Wheeler Large Print Softcover.

The text of this Large Print edition is unabridged.
Other aspects of the book may vary from the original edition.

Set in 16 pt. Plantin by Carleen Stearns.

Printed in the United States on permanent paper.

**Library of Congress Cataloging-in-Publication Data**

Cartland, Barbara, 1902–
    Looking for love / Barbara Cartland.
    Published: Waterville, Me. : Wheeler Pub., 2004.
       p. cm.
    ISBN 1-58724-826-3 (lg. print : sc : alk. paper)
    1. Large type books.   2. Regency fiction.   3. Love stories.
I. Title.
PR6005.A765L58 2004
   823′ .912—dc22                                    2004057228

# Chapter One

## 1803

"Ye're quite certain ye'll be all right, Miss Gilda?"

"Of course I will, Mrs. Hewlett. Do not worry about me, and I hope you enjoy your wedding."

"Oi'm sure Oi shall, Miss. It's reel lucky for our Emily, when her thinks she be on th' shelf, for that farmer t' come along, an' a very nice man he be, too."

Gilda smiled, knowing that Mrs. Hewlett had been worried in case she would have to provide for her niece and was grateful as much for her own sake as Emily's that the "nice farmer" was ready to marry her.

Mrs. Hewlett was the worrying sort and Gilda often thought she was the only person who really cared what became of her now that she was alone after her father's death.

"Now leave everythin' that needs washing up for me when Oi gets back on Monday," Mrs.

Hewlett was saying. "Ye don't want t' trouble yerself t' do anythin' but have a bit o' rest."

That, Gilda thought, was something she had been doing for a long time, and the amount of washing up that would be left after her frugal meals would hardly make a pile even if she did leave it for Mrs. Hewlett.

But she knew it was no use arguing, or Mrs. Hewlett would be worrying about her while she was away in the next village attending Emily's wedding.

Having struggled into a heavy coat even though it was a warm day, Mrs. Hewlett picked up the wicker-basket which she always carried whether there was anything in it or not, and taking a last look round the kitchen lifted the latch of the door.

"Now take care o' yerself, Miss," she admonished, "an Oi'll be back on Monday afternoon if th' stage-coach be punctual, which it's unlikely t' be!"

When the door had closed behind her, Gilda gave a little sigh and, leaving the kitchen, went down the passage to the front of the house.

It was only a short way, for the small Manor in which she had lived ever since she was born had at one time seemed only just large enough for her father, her mother, her sister, and herself.

Now it seemed much too large for one person, and she wondered, as she had been wondering ever since her father had died, whether she should try to sell the house and move into a small cottage.

It would, she thought, be the sensible thing to do. At the same time, she could not bear to part with the furniture, shabby though it was, which she had known all her life and which seemed a part of herself and the only thing she had left.

Her father's desk, her mother's inlaid work-table, and the Chippendale bookcase were all like old friends, and she felt that without them she would be even lonelier than she was already.

At the same time, she had to face facts. She had so little money that she could barely afford to buy enough food to eat unless she could supplement her tiny income in some way.

Her father's pension had died with him. He had served in the Grenadier Guards, and when he was alive his pension as a Major-General had kept them in comparative comfort, or would have done if her father had not amused himself in his old age by investing in stocks and shares.

Gilda could understand the excitement of it, but while the General might have been a very experienced soldier, he knew nothing about finance.

Invariably the companies to which he entrusted his money either went bankrupt or paid such tiny dividends that they were hardly worth the paper on which they were written.

Now all that Gilda had was the very small amount of money her mother had brought into the marriage-settlement, the income from which had been left to the children of the marriage.

Gilda had often wondered what would have happened if her sister had claimed her share.

After Heloise had gone to London to live with her rich Godmother she had shown little or no interest in her impecunious relatives, and Gilda sometimes thought she was ashamed of them.

Sitting now at her father's desk, Gilda pulled open a notebook in which she was trying to jot down all her expenditures.

It seemed to her to come to an uncomfortably large total, despite the fact that she was trying to economise on food, clothing, and in fact everything that was personal.

One economy she had thought of was to dispense with the services of Mrs. Hewlett, but when she had actually suggested this, Mrs. Hewlett had been horrified to the point of being insulted and had even offered to work for nothing.

"Oi've come here for nigh on ten years," she said, "and if ye think ye can do without me now, Miss Gilda, ye're very much mistaken. What's more, yer dear mother'd turn in her grave, she would, at the very idea!"

Mrs. Hewlett had been so voluble on the subject that Gilda felt it was impossible for her

10

to say any more, and she also admitted to herself that without Mrs. Hewlett's incessant good humour she would be very lonely indeed.

In fact, there would be no-one to talk to at all except the Vicar, who was growing very deaf, on an occasional visit, and old Gibbs the gardener.

He was long past work but came because he liked to potter round the place where he had worked for so long and could not bear to see his labours being stifled by weeds or obliterated by overgrown brambles.

Gilda added up the total of what she had spent, checked it again, and knew there was no mistake. It was too much.

"What can I do?" she asked herself.

She wondered whether she had any talent which could bring her some money.

She was well educated compared with many other young women of her age. Her mother, who came from a Cornish family which had held very distinguished posts in the County for many generations, had seen to that.

The fact that her grandfather and great-grandfather and the generations before them had been High Sheriffs, Judges, and even Lords Lieutenant, did not, Gilda thought, make her own brains any the more marketable.

Her father too had been an intelligent man.

His contemporaries who had visited him when he was alive always told Gilda that no General had more skill in deploying his troops

11

or a better grasp of tactics in battle.

"Your father could always be relied on to inflict the maximum losses on the enemy with the minimum to his own men," one of his brother Officers had told Gilda.

She had realised that this was high praise, but it did not solve her own problem.

"I shall have to do something . . . I must!" she said to herself, and rose from the desk to walk to the window.

The Manor stood back from the small country road down which it was nearly a mile to the village. It had a short drive to a gate that was badly in need of repair, while the gravel sweep in front of the house was overgrown with weeds.

Gilda, however, saw only the daffodils under the ancient trees, the lilacs white and purple just coming into bloom, and the first buds on the almond tree which by next week would be a poem of pink and white petals.

'If only I could paint,' she thought, 'I could paint a picture that everybody would want to buy!'

But she knew she could not afford either the canvass or the paints, so the only person who could enjoy the miracle of spring would be herself.

Because the sunshine seemed to call her, she thought the accounts could wait and the best thing she could do would be to go into the garden.

There was plenty of work for her to do there, not only amongst the flowers and shrubs but in the kitchen-garden, where unless she weeded the vegetables and planted those that she would want later in the year, she would be very hungry indeed.

At the same time, she wanted to look more closely at the white lilacs which her mother had always loved and which, if she picked some and placed them in a chest in the Hall, would scent the whole house.

There was a smile on her lips as she turned to leave the window. Then as she did so she looked down the drive and was suddenly still.

To her astonishment she saw coming through the gate a pair of well-bred horses.

Then she saw that the coachman driving them was wearing a cockaded high hat, and incredibly there was a footman beside him.

No-one in the County who was grand enough to have a footman on the box was likely to call, and as the horses drew nearer Gilda thought there must be some mistake and whoever was arriving must be coming to the wrong house.

As they came nearer still, she could see that the horses were drawing a very elegant travelling-carriage with a coat-of-arms painted on the door.

"There is a mistake," Gilda said to herself. "I must tell them so."

As the carriage drew up outside the front

door, she hurried from the Sitting-Room, patting her hair into place as she did so, and conscious that she was wearing one of her oldest cotton gowns which had been washed until the colour had faded and it was too tight and too short.

However, it was of no consequence, for the visitor would not be for her, and when there was a loud rat-tat on the knocker she opened the door, feeling not embarrassed but curious.

A footman, resplendent in a liveried coat embellished with crested silver buttons, was outside.

However, he was not waiting to ask whose house it was, but turned back to open the carriage-door.

Then Gilda gave a little cry of surprise, for stepping out was a vision in blue silk taffeta with a lovely face framed by a bonnet surmounted by ostrich feathers of the same colour.

"Louise!" Gilda exclaimed, then quickly corrected herself. "Heloise!"

After she went to London her sister had changed her name to one that she thought was more unusual and more aristocratic. She had written to her father saying that in the future she was to be addressed as "Heloise."

"I am thrilled to see you!" Gilda said. "But you did not let me know you would be coming."

Heloise bent forward so that Gilda could kiss her cheek.

"I did not know myself until the last moment," she replied.

She turned to the footman.

"Take my trunk upstairs, James," she said in an authoritative voice, "and make sure you return here early on Monday morning. You are not to be late. Do you understand?"

"I understands, Miss."

He started to loosen the cords that bound the trunk to the back of the carriage.

Before Gilda could tell him to which room to take them, Heloise said:

"As Mama's room is the best, that is where I wish to sleep. Tell someone to show him the way."

"Yes, of course," Gilda replied, "but Mrs. Hewlett is not here today."

"Then you will have to show him yourself," Heloise answered, "and make sure that he undoes the straps and opens the lid before he leaves."

"I will do that," Gilda agreed.

Heloise walked into the Sitting-Room and Gilda waited in the Hall until James came in through the front door carrying her sister's trunk.

Then she went ahead of him up the stairs to open the door of the room which her mother had always used and which had been shut up after her father's death.

Hastily Gilda pulled back the curtains and opened the windows.

The room was clean, since Mrs. Hewlett "turned out" every room in the house regularly whether they were used or not.

There was a Holland cover over the bed, which Gilda removed as the footman set down the trunk near the door.

" 'Twill be all right 'ere, Miss?" he asked.

"Yes, thank you," Gilda replied, and thought that if it was not to Heloise's liking she would move it for her.

She noticed that the footman looked round the room with a somewhat contemptuous air, as if he saw how shabby and worn everything was and compared it very unfavourably with the house in which he was employed.

Then unexpectedly he grinned at Gilda and said:

"Nice to be in th' country, Miss. I were brought up on a farm meself an' often misses it."

"I am sure you do," Gilda answered. "London must be very hot and dusty in the summer."

" 'Tis all o' that, an' thick wi' mud in th' winter. Good-day, Miss."

He grinned at her again before she heard his footsteps running down the stairs, and, thinking that Heloise would want her, she hurriedly followed him.

By the time she reached the Hall the carriage was driving away, and she went into the Sitting-Room with a look of apprehension in her blue eyes.

"I am so very . . . very glad to see you, dearest," she said, "but why are you here?"

Her sister had taken off her bonnet and Gilda saw that there was a blue band round her head, while her golden hair curled riotously round her oval forehead.

It was as lovely as the face beneath it and very elegant, as was the gown of white muslin with a high waist and blue ribbons which crossed over her breasts and hung down the back.

"You look lovely . . . simply lovely!" Gilda said impulsively, and Heloise smiled at the compliment.

"I am glad you think so, and the reason I am here is to make somebody say to me exactly what you have just said."

Gilda looked puzzled and Heloise said:

"I have run away — I have disappeared — but the question is, will he or will he not worry as to what has happened to me?"

Heloise was sitting on the sofa and Gilda sat down on the edge of an armchair opposite her.

"You are talking in riddles," she said. "Explain to me . . . tell me exactly what is happening."

Heloise gave a little laugh.

"It is quite simple," she said. "Somehow I have got to bring a certain gentleman 'up to scratch,' and this is the only way I could think of that had anything original about it!"

"Oh, Heloise, how exciting! And what do you think this gentleman will do when he finds you are gone?"

"That is the question," Heloise replied. "He was to have driven me to Ranelagh this afternoon. I was to have dined at his house this evening at a dinner-party where a great number of people will ask why I am not present."

"Have you told him you will be here?" Gilda asked.

"No, of course not! How can you be so stupid? I have just vanished into thin air."

"Oh, Heloise, I think it is very brave of you!" Gilda cried. "But will your Godmother not tell him where you have gone?"

"I took no chances of his coaxing my address out of her," Heloise replied. "I left her a note which my maid will have read to her when she was called this morning."

Gilda looked puzzled and Heloise said:

"Oh, I forgot to tell you. Her Ladyship has an affliction of the eyes which has made her blind."

"Blind!" Gilda exclaimed. "How terrible! What is wrong?"

"The Doctors, who are fools anyway, think it is only a temporary blindness," Heloise said impatiently, "but her eyes are bandaged so that everything has to be read to her. It is my duty as a rule and a very boring one."

"I am so sorry for her."

"Keep your sympathy for me, because I need it," Heloise answered. "Oh, Gilda, if my des-

18

perate gamble does not come off I shall be in despair."

"Are you so much . . . in love with . . . this gentleman?" Gilda asked.

"In love?" Heloise repeated. "That really has little to do with it! I want more than I have ever wanted anything in my whole life to be the Marchioness of Staverton."

"That is the name of the gentleman from whom you are hiding?" Gilda asked.

"Yes, of course," Heloise answered. "Do not be nitwitted, Gilda! Try to understand what is happening. He has been paying court to me in his own way for over a month. I have been waiting, feeling certain two weeks ago that he intended to propose, but . . ."

"What happened?" Gilda interrupted.

"He paid me compliments — he sent me flowers — he has taken me driving — he has given dinner-parties for me."

She paused before she said impressively:

"He has even on two occasions asked me to dance with him, and you have no idea what an honour that was! He hates dancing, and I thought then that I had finally caught him — but no, the words I want to hear have never passed his lips."

Gilda clasped her hands together.

"Oh, Heloise, I can understand how frustrating it must be for you."

"Very, very frustrating!" Heloise agreed. "I have dozens of admirers, really dozens, but

19

none of them measure up to the Marquis."

"Tell me about him."

Heloise gave a sigh.

"He is one of the wealthiest men in the *Beau Monde*. He is a close friend of the Prince of Wales. He is a Corinthian and a Beau, although he does not like one to say he is. And his possessions — oh, Gilda, I cannot begin to describe them!"

"Why has he not been married before?"

"You may well ask," Heloise replied. "He has every girl in London at his feet, or, if they are married, women in his arms!"

Gilda looked shocked and Heloise laughed, but the sound had no humour in it.

"He is not such a fool to make love to an unmarried girl, otherwise her father would pretty soon march him up the aisle!"

The way Heloise spoke was sharp and, Gilda thought, unpleasant.

"I expect," she said a little hesitatingly, "the Marquis has been waiting to . . . fall in love . . . and that is what he must have done . . . with you."

"That is what I thought the moment we first met," Heloise replied, "but it is taking him a long time to say so, far too long for my liking."

"And now that you have disappeared you think that he will realise how much you matter to him?"

"That is what I have come here for," Heloise

said. "In fact, that is what he must do, damn him!"

Gilda gave a little start.

It was strange and very shocking to hear her sister swear.

However, she was too wise to say so, and after a moment she said:

"I am sure, Heloise, it is very remiss of me, but I never asked you if you would like refreshments after your journey."

"Now that you mention it," Heloise answered, "I am thirsty. Is there any wine in this benighted place?"

Gilda looked startled.

"There may be a bottle of claret in the cellar. I have really never looked since Papa died."

"I suppose not," Heloise said. "I cannot imagine you drinking anything but milk or water."

The way she spoke did not sound like a compliment, and Gilda said:

"There is tea if you would like some."

"I suppose I shall have to if there is nothing else!" Heloise said. "But it must be nearly luncheon-time. Have you something decent to eat?"

Gilda thought quickly.

"There are eggs, so I could make you an omelette, or there is some cold ham which Mrs. Hewlett brought me which her son who has the farm next door had cured."

Heloise wrinkled her nose.

"It does not sound very appetising. You had

better make me the omelette. If nothing else, I suppose a starvation diet is good for my figure."

Gilda made no answer to this. Instead she picked up the blue silk travelling-cape which Heloise had thrown down on a chair and carried it into the Hall.

She hung it up in the carved oak cupboard which contained two of her father's overcoats and a rather disreputable cloak she wore in the garden when it was cold.

As she hung Heloise's cape beside them she was conscious that it exuded a fragrance which she was sure came from Paris.

Then she hurried into the kitchen and started preparing the omelette.

It took her a little time to build up the fire in the stove, which had begun to die down after Mrs. Hewlett had left, to boil a kettle for the tea, then to heat the frying-pan for the omelette.

There were three eggs in the larder, which she broke into a bowl, thinking as she did so that she would have to go to the farm to get some more for Heloise's dinner and certainly for her breakfast tomorrow morning.

She was mixing the eggs when Heloise came into the kitchen.

She looked so lovely that for a moment Gilda could only stare at her, thinking that with her fashionably dressed golden hair and her blue eyes she was like the Goddess of Spring.

22

"It looks just the same," Heloise said disparagingly. "I had forgotten how small and shabby the house was. How you can stand it, Gilda, I do not know!"

"I have had no choice," Gilda answered. "In fact, I have been wondering what I should do, because quite frankly, Heloise, I cannot afford to live even here."

As she spoke she saw her sister stiffen, and she knew instinctively that Heloise was afraid she was going to ask her for money.

"What did Papa leave you?" Heloise asked after a moment.

"His pension died with him," Gilda replied. "If Mama had lived she would of course have been entitled to a widow's pension, but children are not provided for."

"I expect if they are boys they are expected to earn their own living, and if they are girls to get married," Heloise said. "That is what you will have to do."

Gilda laughed.

"An opportunity would be a fine thing! The only unmarried man in the village is the Vicar and he is over seventy."

"If you married him at least you would have some money!" Heloise remarked.

Gilda laughed again, but she had the uncomfortable idea that Heloise was not intending to be funny.

Her sister sat down on a kitchen chair and looked at her.

"You know, Gilda," she said after a moment, "we are not unalike. If you took a little more trouble with yourself, you might easily attract some country squire, but that gown you are wearing is a disgrace!"

"I know," Gilda said humbly, "but the last thing I can afford is clothes, and it would be no use being smartly dressed if I have to starve to death."

"Are things really as bad as that?"

"They are worse."

Heloise sighed.

"I suppose I could have brought you some of my gowns which I have no further use for. One thing about Her Ladyship is that, although she is a bore to live with, she is very generous in wanting me to look my best."

"Surely she has been very, very kind to you," Gilda said. "After all, it was her idea that you should go to live with her when Mama died."

There was a moment's silence. Then Heloise said:

"Actually, it was mine!"

Gilda put down the fork she held in her hand with a clatter.

"Your idea?" she exclaimed. "Do you mean . . . are you really telling me . . . ?"

"I wrote to her," Heloise interrupted. "She is my Godmother, and I saw, as no-one else did, that if I lived here in this hole I might as well be buried alive."

"But . . . how could you be so . . . daring?" Gilda asked.

"Nothing ventured, nothing gained!" Heloise replied. "I wrote her a pathetic letter, one that would have brought tears to the eyes of a stone-image, saying how much I missed Mama, how poor and deprived I was, and how Papa did not want me."

"Oh, Heloise, how could you tell such lies? You know Papa adored you. After all, you were the first baby, and Mama always said it was the most wonderful moment of their married life when you were born, and they thought you were a gift from God."

"Well, as God was not very generous when it came to the things I wanted," Heloise replied, "I had to take things into my own hands."

"You have certainly been very successful about it."

"It was clever of me, was it not?" Heloise said. "Actually it is very nice for Godmama to have me with her. She has had to admit herself that because I am such a success in London, far more interesting and distinguished people come to the house than if I were not there."

"But it is still very kind of her to give you lovely clothes and make it possible for you to go to the Balls and parties. You used to write and tell me about them when you first left."

"I have had no time to write now," Heloise said quickly. "There is never a moment when I am not being entertained, fêted, and of course made love to by attractive men."

"I am not a bit surprised," Gilda said. "You were always beautiful, but never as beautiful as you are now."

The note of sincerity in her voice was very touching, and Heloise preened herself before she said:

"You are right, Gilda. I do look my best, but sometimes I get tired when there is a Ball every night and so many delightful things to do in the daytime."

"But how do you manage since Her Ladyship is blind and cannot chaperone you?"

"I write letters to her friends asking them to chaperone me," Heloise replied, "but what more often happens is that invitations to the big dinner-parties and Balls come from people who are well aware of her affliction and therefore they take it for granted that they will look after me."

"It must be very exciting for you to be such a success."

There was a pause before Heloise said in a hard voice:

"This is my third Season, and I have to be married! No beauty, however much acclaimed, lasts forever, and I intend that the Marquis shall *marry* me."

She accentuated the word so that it sounded positively aggressive, and Gilda said in a small voice:

"Suppose he does not?"

"I have an alternative," Heloise replied, "but not nearly such an attractive one."

"Who is he?"

"Nobody of great importance, except that he is extremely wealthy. But I refuse to consider him. I can see myself only as the Marchioness of Staverton, and that is what I intend to be!"

Again she spoke in a way that made Gilda look at her apprehensively.

She thought that as Heloise was so lovely it spoilt her when she spoke in a hard voice that seemed somehow to vibrate through the kitchen and jar on the sunshine coming through the window.

She had beaten the eggs and now she said:

"I suppose you will want to eat in the Dining-Room?"

As she spoke she took a tray from one of the shelves.

"Of course," Heloise replied. "Although I am sure you eat in the kitchen when you are alone, I am not sinking to that level!"

"No . . . of course not," Gilda said humbly. "Go into the Dining-Room, Heloise, and everything will be ready for you in a moment."

She put some knives and forks on the tray and a plate at the front of the stove to warm, then started to make the omelette.

She knew there would not be enough for two, and thought she would take in a piece of the ham for herself in case Heloise did not wish to eat alone.

Then she thought it was unlikely that her sister would notice what she was eating.

She remembered that although it seemed unkind, she had often thought when Heloise was living at home that as far as she was concerned no-one else existed in the whole world except her.

"It is understandable because she is so beautiful," Gilda had excused her sister's selfishness then, and she was thinking the same now.

As she skilfully tipped the beautifully browned omelette onto the warm plate, she found herself wondering if Heloise would be happy when she had attained her desire and married her Marquis.

She supposed that wealth and position and a leading role in Society would bring happiness to some people, although it was not anything she wanted herself.

'When I marry,' Gilda thought, 'I want a man who will love me and whom I will love, and we will be content to be together, whether our home is a very grand one or a very poor one like this.'

She remembered how happy her mother had been with her father when he was not away with his Regiment and after he had retired.

The General had been a lot older than his wife and they had not had children until they had been married for some years. Gilda could only vaguely remember days when they had followed their father to Salisbury

Plain and other Army depots.

Once he had gone abroad for two years, and when he returned her mother had been so happy it had seemed to Gilda as a little girl that every day was like a Fête Day.

Then when there were no more journeyings and they had settled down at the Manor, she could remember how content her father and mother had been in the garden or reading together in the Study.

There had been laughter at meal-times, and before she became old enough to go down to dinner, Gilda could remember listening at the top of the stairs to the chatter of voices in the Dining-Room.

Afterwards there had been the sound of music coming from the Drawing-Room as her mother played and sang old songs to which her father liked to listen.

"They were happy," Gilda told herself, "and that is what Heloise should want, not just material things."

But she knew her sister would never listen to her if she tried to explain the difference. Anyway, she doubted if she would understand.

Heloise had always craved for luxuries and for all the things that money could buy.

She remembered her sister on her fifteenth birthday, when she herself had been thirteen, stamping her foot because her presents were not what she wanted.

"I asked Mama for a new gown," she said angrily, "and a coat trimmed with fur! All she has given me is this rubbish!"

As she spoke she had thrown across the room a pretty bonnet trimmed with blue ribbons with a small reticule to match and a pair of satin slippers.

"But they are so pretty!" Gilda had expostulated. "And you know you needed some new slippers."

"I also wanted a new gown and a new coat!" Heloise had raged.

"I do not think Mama can afford those things at the moment," Gilda said.

"Well, she could have sold something to get me what I want," Heloise retorted. "I think Mama is selfish and beastly, and I hate my nasty dull presents!"

Gilda had been shocked at the time, but she had not been surprised when a month later Heloise had coaxed and wheedled what she wanted out of her mother, although later she had said to Gilda:

"We shall have to economise, Gilda, to make up for the things I have bought Louise. But they have made her happy, so I can easily go without a new coat myself this winter."

Yes, Heloise had always been the same, Gilda thought as she carried the omelette to the Dining-Room.

Although she had nothing to do but sit and wait, Heloise had made no attempt to lay the table-cloth, and now as Gilda quickly arranged

30

it for her she sat back in her father's arm-chair and looked almost disdainfully at the om-elette.

"Is this what you call a square meal?" she asked. "It is lucky that I am prepared to admit that it will do me good to fast for the next forty-eight hours, for it is very difficult not to over-eat in London."

"Is the food superb?" Gilda asked, aware that Heloise was ready to gossip.

"It is when one dines with the Prince of Wales."

"Do you mean to say that you have dined with him?"

"Yes, I have, and I am quite certain it was the Marquis who made him invite me. He is always curious about anybody new who is beautiful, although he is not really interested in young girls."

She paused to note that Gilda was listening intently and went on:

"And when I received my invitation I was naturally overjoyed."

"I am sure you were," Gilda agreed.

"It was a terrible rush to get a new gown, and as I said to Godmama, I could hardly go in the old rags I was wearing at the time."

"Was that not rather rude, when she had given them to you?"

"Not at all! She agreed," Heloise said care-lessly, "and sent me to the very best dressmaker in Bond Street. It cost a great amount of money, but it was worth it to have the Prince paying me compliments, as did every other man of consequence who was at the dinner."

"But did that not make the Marquis jealous?"

There was a frown on Heloise's small white forehead before she replied:

"I am not certain — and this is the truth, Gilda — what he really feels about me."

She stopped eating for a moment before she said:

"He is the most infuriating, exasperating man I have ever met in my whole life. One never knows what he is thinking or feeling."

"Then why do you want to marry him?"

"Do not be so silly! I have answered that question once!" Heloise answered sharply.

"Yes, of course . . . I am sorry," Gilda said quickly. "But he sounds frightening."

"He does not frighten me," Heloise said. "He just makes me very angry and very frustrated, but I will get his ring on my finger or die in the attempt."

"Do you really think you will be happy when you are married to such a man? Suppose he continues to upset you?"

Heloise shrugged her shoulders.

"It will be too late then for him to do anything about it, and though you do not know it living here in the back of beyond, most couples in the *Beau Monde* each go their own way."

Gilda looked surprised and Heloise went on:

"I am sure that after the first year, when I

suppose I shall have to produce an heir to the title, I shall have my friends and the Marquis will have his, and neither of us will ask too many questions."

There was silence for a moment. Then Gilda said:

"Do you mean that he will have . . . lady-friends?"

"Of course I mean that," Heloise replied. "He would be a monk or a Saint if he remained faithful to one woman, and I have every intention of keeping my admirers happy until I am a ripe old age."

Gilda wondered exactly what this entailed, but she was too nervous to ask. Instead, as Heloise finished her omelette she took away her empty plate, saying:

"I am afraid there is nothing else except cheese."

"I hate cheese!" Heloise said petulantly.

"I will try to get something better for you this evening, and I will cook you a pudding. Do you still like treacle tart?"

"Good Heavens! I had forgotten such things existed!" Heloise exclaimed. "But now that you speak of it, I remember when we used to have treacle tart one day, plum duff the next, and roly-poly pudding the third. How we ever endured such horrors I cannot imagine!"

"Tell me what you eat in London," Gilda said, to change the subject.

Soon Heloise was expatiating on the delicious dishes that she had enjoyed in distinguished houses.

At the same time, she made it very clear that once she had the Marquis's Chef under her orders, the food that would be served in any house of which she was châtelaine would exceed anything she had enjoyed at anyone else's.

They talked, or rather Heloise did, all through the afternoon, and only when she said she would lie down for a little while before supper did Gilda have the chance to hurry to the nearest farm, which was owned by Mrs. Hewlett's son.

As she went, she calculated what it would cost to buy a small leg of lamb for Heloise's dinner.

She would also want eggs, and if she was fortunate Farmer Hewlett might have made some sausage-meat, which Heloise used to enjoy when she lived at home.

Gilda knew that all these things would come to a considerable amount of money, and although she knew it was wrong of her, she could not help feeling a little relieved that Heloise did not intend to stay long.

She was quite certain that she would not offer to pay for anything while she was at home.

Although it was exciting to see her again and hear all the things she had to tell her, Gilda was a little hurt that this was the first time she had heard from Heloise for over a year.

It was quite obvious that while she was in

London she had forgotten her sister and her shabby home and was completely absorbed in her new life.

'She is very lucky, and Lady Neyland has been so kind to her,' Gilda thought.

She wished that Heloise did not sound so bored by her Godmother's blindness and so ungrateful for all she had received from somebody who was not even a relative.

Lady Neyland had in fact been a close friend of her mother's before she married, and although they had seen each other only spasmodically in the years that followed Mrs. Wyngate's marriage, they had continued to correspond.

Because Lady Neyland had no children, she had always been interested in her friend's family. Presents had come at Christmas for both girls and Heloise had always received something on her birthday.

"It is a pity my Godparents died when I was young and omitted to remember me in their wills," Gilda said to herself with a faint smile.

Then she told herself it would be very wrong to be jealous of Heloise.

It was her sister's right to have the best that was available, and she had been very happy for the last two years after her mother's death when she had been alone with her father.

She loved listening to him talk about his life in the Army and they read interesting books together.

Thinking back, she knew that not even the

Balls that Heloise described so vividly could make up for their companionship, which she found difficult to put into words but which had enriched her life.

"I loved Papa and he loved me," Gilda told herself.

That meant a great deal more than pursuing a Marquis who, if she was honest, she thought sounded extremely unpleasant.

# Chapter Two

Heloise had decided to spend most of Sunday in bed, and Gilda had carried first her breakfast upstairs at a very late hour, then her luncheon.

She had cooked the lamb very carefully, and Heloise, having eaten two helpings, had actually said that she found it tender.

Now she sat up in bed looking exceedingly beautiful and was ready to talk.

"I am so glad you had such a good night," Gilda said. "You must have been very tired to sleep so late."

Heloise laughed.

"It was not so much being tired as taking an extra-large dose of laudanum."

Gilda was horrified.

"Laudanum!" she exclaimed. "You know Mama always disapproved when the Doctor used to suggest that Papa should take a spoonful at night when his rheumatism was bad."

"I could not sleep without it."

Gilda was looking disapproving and Heloise continued:

"It is all very well for you to criticise, but if you were dancing until three or four o'clock in the morning and drinking champagne, when you did get to bed you would find it impossible to get to sleep."

Gilda could not help feeling that she would like to try the experience of dancing until the early hours, but she felt it was important that Heloise should realise that laudanum was bad for her.

"I am sure you would find it easy to sleep if you drank some warm milk. Mama always said honey and milk . . ."

"Oh, do not fuss!" Heloise interrupted sharply. "I want to tell you what a success I was at the Ball given by the Duchess of Bedford. Everybody said I looked sensational, and it was after that that the Marquis began to pay me attention."

She was back again talking about the Marquis, although Gilda had no wish to complain.

She found it fascinating to listen to Heloise's descriptions of the Balls she had attended, the compliments she had received, and her descriptions of her best gowns, which cost more money than she herself had to live on for a whole year.

She was not jealous of her sister and never had been. Heloise had always taken first place in her father's affections and in everything they had done as children.

It was true that she was eighteen months older than Gilda. At the same time, she was so beautiful that it seemed to be her right to be given the best of everything that was available, and for Gilda to be content with what was left over.

"When the Marquis said to me," Heloise was saying now, " 'I will give a dinner-party for you at my house in Berkeley Square,' I knew I was being specially favoured."

"Is that the party to which you did not go last night?" Gilda asked.

Heloise nodded.

"Surely that will make him very angry?"

"It will make him jealous," Heloise replied. "He will be quite certain I am doing something which I find more amusing and attractive than dining with him, and the mere idea will give him a shock."

Gilda could not help thinking that it was very bad manners for her sister to run away at the last moment and without notice from an entertainment which had been specially provided in her honour, but she was too wise to say so.

"The trouble with the Marquis," Heloise went on, "is that he is spoilt. He has everything he wants in the world, and from all I hear, no woman has ever refused him her favours or anything else he asked of her."

She said this in a voice which surprised Gilda

and made her wonder what exactly her sister meant.

But before she could ask questions Heloise continued:

"I worked it out in my own mind that the one thing which would really make the Marquis consider me more seriously than he has done up to now is for me to appear reluctant to be with him and not pressure him in the same way that every other woman does."

She laughed before she added:

"Of course I am in fact doing so! I am determined to catch him and make sure he does not get away."

"And when you have caught him?" Gilda asked.

"Then I will be the Marchioness of Staverton and my worries will be over."

Gilda smiled.

"Have you really any worries? You certainly do not look troubled."

"Of course I am worried," Heloise said. "I have told you I have to be married. I shall be twenty, as you well know, in July, and most girls who were débutantes at the same time as I was have already found husbands."

There was a little frown between her blue eyes as she went on:

"But they were so lucky. They had fathers and mothers who arranged marriages for them, as is usual in aristocratic circles."

"But could not your Godmother . . . arrange

a . . . marriage for . . . you?" Gilda asked hesitatingly.

She thought as she spoke that an arranged marriage sounded a very cold, almost unpleasant way of being married.

But if it was the customary thing to do, then of course it was something Heloise would want.

"Godmama is so stupid!" Heloise replied contemptuously. "She really does not understand what is expected of her. When I suggested last year that she might approach Lord Cornwall, whose eldest son was interested in me for a short while, she said it was too embarrassing as she did not know the Cornwalls!"

"I can understand her feelings."

"You would, because you are as stupid as she is," Heloise retorted, "and I daresay that Mama if she were alive would have been no better. One does not have to be sentimental when it comes to social advancement."

Gilda was silent for a moment. Then she said:

"Is the Marquis expecting to have an arranged marriage?"

"I am sure he has been approached by every Duke and Duchess and every Earl and Countess who want to push their plain daughters off onto him," Heloise said. "But I am quite certain he wishes to choose his own wife."

"Then we must just pray that he chooses you," Gilda said.

"It is not prayers which are needed at the

moment, but intelligence," Heloise answered, "and that is what I have. I am sure by this time the Marquis is wondering frantically what has happened to me and whom I am with."

"Will you tell him you have been here?"

"You must be crazy!" Heloise replied. "I shall look down my nose and say I have had a delightful time. If I speak in a soft, rather passionate little voice, he will think somebody has been making love to me and kissing me. That will make him jealous, and then anything might happen!"

She lay back against the pillows and turned her blue eyes up to the ceiling as if she was thinking ecstatically of what it would mean when the Marquis proposed to her.

Gilda did not speak for a moment. Then she said:

"Of course I am very . . . ignorant about such things . . . but would the Marquis not think you were rather . . . fast if you allowed men to . . . kiss you?"

"He would think it very strange if no-one wished to!" Heloise replied.

"I can understand their wanting to," Gilda said. "You are so lovely, dearest, that I am sure every man finds you irresistible, but . . . should you kiss them?"

"You do not know what you are talking about," Heloise said. "Just leave me to get the Marquis in my own way. I know what I am doing."

"Yes . . . of course," Gilda said humbly.

When it was tea-time, Heloise decided she was far too comfortable in bed to move, so Gilda brought her tea upstairs.

She arranged her mother's best china on the tray with a pretty lace cloth and hoped Heloise would enjoy the shortbread biscuits that she had hastily baked while the oven was still hot.

When tea was finished she said in a small, rather shy voice:

"I have . . . something to . . . ask you, Heloise."

"What is it?" her sister enquired.

"If I came to London . . . would it be . . . possible for you to find me . . . employment of some . . . sort?"

Heloise sat up abruptly.

"Come to London? What would you want to come to London for?" she demanded.

"I have been . . . thinking things over," Gilda said. "I really cannot afford to stay here . . . unless I earn money somehow . . . but I cannot . . . think what I can . . . do."

"What do you expect to do in London?" Heloise asked.

She spoke aggressively and Gilda thought uncomfortably that her eyes looked hostile.

"I . . . wondered if it would be . . . possible for me to . . . give lessons to . . . children or to . . . look after them."

"Do you mean become a Governess?" Heloise asked in tones of horror.

"Well . . . something like . . . that."

"How do you think I would feel," Heloise enquired, "with my sister nothing more or less than a superior servant? How can you suggest anything so abominable?"

"I am . . . sorry," Gilda replied. "I did not . . . think it would . . . upset you."

"Of course it upsets me!" Heloise snapped. "I am a Lady of Fashion, and naturally I have never admitted to anybody that my home is a crumbling, tumble-down Manor and my father had no money except what he earned as a soldier."

Gilda thought uncomfortably that she had often suspected that Heloise was ashamed of her family. But now that she put it into words, it came as a shock that made her clasp her fingers together because they were trembling.

"I am . . . sorry, Heloise," she said quickly. "I did not mean to . . . upset you. I will manage . . . somehow."

As she spoke she thought of how last night she had looked at her cash-book again and knew it was really impossible to live at the Manor on the small amount she could draw from her mother's money.

"If you have to teach children, you can teach them here!" Heloise said in a hard voice.

"There is already a teacher in the village," Gilda replied. "It is only a Penny School, and I am afraid poor Miss Crew would starve to death if she had not a little money of her own."

There was silence. Then Heloise said:

"I have told you, you will have to get married. There must be a farmer or perhaps even a well-to-do tradesman who would think it an honour to have you as his wife."

Gilda rose from the bed and walked to the window.

She stood there not looking out at the afternoon sunshine and the overgrown garden, but fighting back the tears that came into her eyes.

Now she knew exactly what Heloise thought of her and that she had no affection either for her or for her mother's memory.

To suggest that she should marry a farmer or tradesman rather than become a nuisance showed all too clearly the contempt that Gilda had always felt in her heart Heloise really had for her.

Her mother had always been proud of her distinguished Cornish ancestry, and her father's family had all served their country either as soldiers or sailors for generations.

Her grandfather who had been a General had been Knighted, and her great-grandfather had his place in the history-books.

As Gilda fought back her tears, a voice from the bed said:

"I suppose what it comes down to is that I shall have to give you some money, although I do think it is extremely tiresome that you should want it."

Gilda turned from the window.

45

"It is . . . all right, Heloise," she said. "I will
. . . manage somehow."

Heloise, however, was not listening.

She looked so cross and disagreeable that it
spoilt her pink and white and gold beauty, and
for a moment she looked exactly as she had
when as a small girl she flew into a tantrum
whenever she could not get her own way.

"I tell you what I will do," she said. "I will
give you twenty pounds a year until you are
married, and it will be no use whining for any
more."

"I am not . . . whining," Gilda said.

She tried to speak proudly, but her voice
broke on the words and two tears ran down her
cheeks.

"I will give it to you," Heloise went on as if
Gilda had not spoken, "but on the condition
that you do not come to London, nor do you
ever at any time make any other claims upon
me."

"I would . . . certainly not do . . . that."

"What I mean," Heloise went on, "is that
when I marry the Marquis I shall not tell him I
have a sister, nor are you at any time to appear
in my life or ever to tell people outside the village that we are related."

"I promise I will do that," Gilda said, "but,
Heloise, I will not take your money. In fact,
after what you have just said, I would rather
scrub other people's door-steps than accept a
penny from you!"

She walked out of the bedroom as she spoke, shutting the door behind her. Then she ran to her own room to fling herself down on her bed and burst into tears.

Because Heloise was the last member of her family left, she had always thought of her with warmth and love, but now as she lay there she knew that that feeling was more imaginary than real.

She had imagined herself into thinking that she loved Heloise and Heloise loved her, simply because without that love she was completely and utterly alone.

Now that she knew exactly what Heloise felt about her, it was as if she had lost something precious and it had left a void in her life which nothing could heal.

She cried for a long time.

Then she realised that Heloise would soon be wanting dinner and she must cook the ox-tongue which Farmer Hewlett had persuaded her to buy.

"Oi won't charge ye much fer it, Miss Gilda," he said. "An' it'll be a nice mouthful for the two o' ye."

Gilda had thanked him, and now she remembered that she had told Farmer Hewlett that she had a visitor but fortunately she had not said it was her sister.

She had felt he would not be interested as his mother would have been, and anyway she had been in a hurry and had just bought the lamb and the eggs and had only added the tongue when he insisted.

She washed her face in cold water and went downstairs.

All the time that she was cooking she was wondering despairingly how she would be able to manage when Heloise had gone and the tithes on the Manor soon became due.

"Perhaps I was silly to refuse the offer of twenty pounds she made me," she told herself.

Then she thought of her Cornish ancestors and lifted her chin.

She had been born with the same pride with which they had carried their arms into battle first against the Normans, then against the Barons who had threatened their freedom.

"I will manage . . . of course I will manage," Gilda told herself.

She felt a little embarrassed when she carried Heloise's tray upstairs, but her sister merely said when she appeared:

"I cannot think why you have been away for so long. I had to light the candles myself."

"I am sorry," Gilda said, "but I have been cooking the supper, and I hope you will enjoy it."

"I expect so," Heloise replied indifferently, "and I hope you had the sense to bring up the bottle of claret you were talking about."

"Oh, I am sorry," Gilda said. "I never thought of it, but do you think claret is good for you? Mama always said that too much wine could ruin a woman's complexion."

"Mama talked a lot of nonsense!" Heloise replied. "I have to drink in London, although some young girls are forbidden to do so by their mothers."

"Then why do you drink?" Gilda asked.

"Because I want to, for one thing," Heloise replied, "and because it makes me enjoy myself more."

"I have always heard that the Prince of Wales drinks a great deal and so do the Bucks and Beaux," Gilda remarked.

"They sometimes get unpleasantly drunk before the end of an evening," Heloise admitted, "but not those who are Corinthians, because they want to be fit for when they are racing."

"I always imagined that the right sort of gentleman would also be athletic," Gilda said.

"Well, that is certainly what the Marquis is," Heloise replied, getting back to her favourite subject. "Because he is so big and tall he has to keep his weight down for the Steeple-Chases he always wins, and they say he is the finest swordsman in the whole of the *Beau Monde*."

"Have you ever seen him fence?"

"No," Heloise replied, "because ladies are very seldom invited to the Gymnasiums where the duellists exercise. Not that I am interested."

"But you must be!" Gilda cried.

"Oh, I pretend to be," Heloise answered, "but I do not want to watch the Marquis doing things. I want to listen to him talking to me and telling me how beautiful I am."

She picked up a hand-mirror which she had beside her on the bed and contemplated her face in it.

As she did so, Gilda said:

"Do you know, Heloise, at the moment . . . you look exactly like Mama. She always said we were both like her and her grandmother, who was a great beauty."

"I do not suppose anybody ever heard of her outside Cornwall," Heloise said scornfully. "I am a rival of Georgina, Duchess of Devonshire! In fact most people think I am more beautiful than she is!"

"I am sure you are," Gilda said loyally.

When the supper was over Heloise said she was going to sleep.

"I want to have a long night tonight because tomorrow I shall be dancing and I want to look my best."

She told Gilda to fetch her another night-gown so that she could change from the one she had worn all day.

She also made her pin her hair into curls round her forehead and became quite angry when at first Gilda did not do it as skilfully as the lady's-maid she had left behind.

"I am sorry," Gilda said, "I am trying to do exactly as you tell me, but it is something I have never done before."

"That is obvious from the mess your own hair is in."

However, Heloise conceded that her lady's-maid had been taught by an experienced hair-dresser what to do before she finally got it right.

"Of course, whenever I am going to a Ball, a *Coiffeur* comes to the house to attend to me," Heloise boasted. "He always says I am a great advertisement for him and everybody wants him because I look so lovely."

Gilda put the last pin into her sister's golden hair.

"Now, is that all right?" she asked.

"Not too bad," Heloise conceded.

On her sister's instructions Gilda put a fine lace cap on her head to hold the pins in place.

Then Heloise anointed her face with a lotion which came from Bond Street.

"It is made from the roots of irises," she said, "and keeps the skin clear and white. It is very, very expensive."

"You have always had a beautiful skin," Gilda replied, "and I do not believe that irises or anything else have much to do with it."

Heloise laughed.

"I am glad Godmama cannot hear you say that," she said. "She complained about the last bill and said that I was too young to need such aids to beauty."

"I am sure she is right," Gilda said. "You do not need any lotions except fresh air and water."

She spoke positively. At the same time, she

did not want Heloise to go away hating her because she was critical.

"After all, whatever she may say, and however much she may be ashamed of me, she is still my sister," Gilda argued with herself, "and perhaps one day — who knows? — she may need me again."

Heloise, who had been sitting on the stool in front of the dressing-table, got into bed.

"Now shut the window," she said to Gilda, "and make quite certain the curtains are properly closed. I do not want the light to wake me."

Gilda obeyed, thinking that the room would be rather stuffy, but she did not wish to argue.

"One last thing," Heloise went on, "bring me my bottle of laudanum. It is on the washing-stand, and I shall want a spoon."

"Oh, Heloise, do not take it!" Gilda begged.

"I have every intention of sleeping from now until eight o'clock tomorrow morning, when you must call me so that I can be ready when the carriage comes," Heloise said.

There was nothing more Gilda could say, and she fetched the bottle from the washing-stand, feeling as she carried it across the room that the dark liquid in it looked sinister.

Heloise took three teaspoonfuls, then when Gilda would have taken it away she said:

"Leave it by the bed. I sometimes find difficulty in getting off to sleep and take another spoonful."

Gilda did as she was told, then blew out one

of the candles by the bed.

"If there is nothing more you want," she said, "I will bring your breakfast up at eight o'clock and pack your trunk."

"If I am drowsy, wake me," Heloise said. "I must be in London before luncheon, as I expect the Marquis will be waiting to see me."

"I hope he is, for your sake."

Gilda blew out the candles on the dressing-table and walked towards the door.

"Good-night, Heloise," she said. "It has been nice for me to have you here, and whatever you may feel about me, I shall always pray for you and hope that you get everything you want in life."

"I will!" Heloise replied firmly.

Gilda went from the bedroom down the stairs to the kitchen.

She had the dinner-plates to wash up and she also laid everything ready on a tray for Heloise's breakfast, thinking as she did so:

'I must try to keep the Manor so that there will be somewhere for Heloise to come if things go wrong.'

She did not know why, but she had the feeling that her sister would not marry the Marquis, however determined she might be to do so.

There were times when Gilda had presentiments about people which were illogical and not based on fact, but invariably they came true.

She knew it was due to her Cornish blood,

53

and her mother had often told her how, like the Scots and the Welsh, the Cornish people were Celts and therefore had instincts which were at times clairvoyant.

"I have always known when your father was in danger," Mrs. Wyngate used to say in her soft voice. "At first I thought it was my imagination, but later when these feelings came I used to jot down the dates and time of day."

Her voice deepened as she continued:

"When your father came home, I found they coincided exactly with the moment when a native spear missed him by a hair's breadth, or he was fighting a battle in which many other soldiers lost their lives."

Gilda had found that she too had this power of clairvoyance.

She always knew when she met people if they were honest and true or twisted and crafty.

She also was invariably aware whether what she was being told was the truth or not.

Afterwards, she thought to herself that because her presentiments were invariably accurate they were extremely embarrassing.

Now when Heloise had been talking of the Marquis and of her conviction that he would propose marriage, Gilda had known it was something he would not do and her sister was doomed to disappointment.

"I am wrong . . . I am sure I am . . . wrong," she tried to tell herself when finally she went to bed.

But as she undressed, her feelings were too strong to be denied.

Because she did not wish to think about them, she pinned her hair into curls as she had pinned Heloise's.

As it happened, Gilda's hair curled naturally, while Heloise's had always been straight.

'If it is too curly in the morning, I shall look like the top of a mop!' Gilda thought.

At the same time, she thought that when she combed her hair out, the fashion would be as becoming to her as it was to Heloise.

She thought of the beautiful gowns her sister had to wear and the bonnet in which she had travelled with its small blue ostrich feathers.

'I wish I could try it on,' she thought, but knew if she asked her sister would refuse.

Heloise had made no further reference to her offer of twenty pounds a year, which Gilda had refused, and in the light of what she had said it was obvious that unless a real crisis occurred, once she had left she would never return.

She also wished to forget that she had a sister.

It hurt, but Gilda told herself she had to be sensible. There was no point in trying to alter people from what they were.

Gilda awoke and realised that she had plenty of time to prepare Heloise's breakfast.

Then she got up and went downstairs to tidy the house and dust the Sitting-Room.

It was something she usually did anyway, leaving the other rooms for Mrs. Hewlett but preferring to handle herself the small chic ornaments her mother had loved instead of trusting them to Mrs. Hewlett's heavy hands.

The fire was burning brightly in the stove by the time she had finished, and she thought that before she cooked the eggs it would be a good idea to call Heloise and make quite certain she was properly awake to enjoy her breakfast.

She therefore went upstairs a few minutes before eight and crept quietly into the room to pull back the curtains.

The sunshine poured in, and glancing out the window Gilda thought there were more blossoms out on the lilac bushes than there had been the day before.

Then she turned towards the bed.

As she had expected, Heloise was fast asleep.

She stood looking at her sister and thought how lovely she was and that she looked very much younger when she was unconscious than when she was awake.

Now there was a faint smile on her lips and her skin seemed almost translucent.

"Heloise!" But there was no response.

Gilda called her name again. Then she bent forward to touch her shoulder.

Her sister did not move.

"Heloise, you must wake up!" Gilda said. "It is eight o'clock, and you know you have to hurry to London to see the Marquis."

She thought that, if nothing else, would arouse her, but still Heloise did not stir.

Then Gilda touched her hand which lay outside the sheets, and when she did so she started.

Heloise's skin was cold, so cold that it was almost like touching a marble statue rather than a human being.

It was then that Gilda glanced at the laudanum bottle which stood beside the bed.

It was not in the same position as where she had put it last night, but was nearer to Heloise, and the spoon which she had wiped after her sister had used it had obviously been used again.

Gilda felt frightened.

Holding Heloise's hand in both of hers, she rubbed it, saying as she did so:

"Wake up, Heloise! Wake up!"

There was no response and Heloise's hand was still cold.

'As cold,' Gilda thought, 'as death!'

It was then that frantically she put both her hands on her sister's shoulders and shook her. As she did so, Heloise's head fell forward limply like that of a rag doll.

It took Gilda some moments to face the truth. Then she knew unmistakably that Heloise was dead.

Because her mother had always called on the villagers when they were ill and Gilda often went with her, she had seen a number of dead people.

Only after she had felt Heloise's heart and pulse and got no response did she wonder desperately what she should do.

There was no Doctor in the village.

She would have to send to the nearest town, which was five miles away, where a young man had taken over the practice of the old Doctor whom Gilda had known since she was a child.

This meant he would have to be paid, and Gilda could not help feeling it would be a waste of money when there was nothing he could do or say except what she knew already, that Heloise had taken an overdose of laudanum.

The laying-out locally was always done by Mrs. Hewlett and she would not be back until the afternoon.

'I will wait until she returns,' Gilda thought. 'Then I will tell the Vicar.'

She then remembered that the Vicar was away and would not be home for nearly three weeks.

That meant that a Clergyman from another village would have to be contacted to perform the burial service.

"How could this have happened?" Gilda asked herself unhappily, and wondered if she could have done anything to prevent it.

She thought again how lovely Heloise looked and how very, very young.

'She is young,' Gilda thought, 'and yet, how much more Heloise has already done in her life than I shall ever do!'

She wondered if many people in London would mourn her sister or whether she would soon be forgotten. Perhaps there would be somebody new, an even more beautiful young girl whom the Beaux would admire and never have another thought for Heloise, who had died when she was not yet twenty.

"It is all the Marquis's fault," Gilda told herself. "If he had proposed to her she would never have come home. She would have stayed in London and been with him and been so happy that she would not have needed laudanum."

The thought of the Marquis made Gilda realise that she would have to tell him and Heloise's Godmother, Lady Neyland, that her sister was dead.

"I will write a letter," she decided, "which can go back with the carriage when it arrives."

She wondered if it would be more polite to go in person to Lady Neyland, as she was blind, to tell her what had happened.

"I am sure that is what Mama would think I should do," Gilda told herself. "And if Lady Neyland would be kind enough to send me back in her carriage, I would be able to return late in the afternoon."

Then she told herself that if she did go to London she had no clothes fit to wear. Although Lady Neyland would be unable to see her, the Marquis might be waiting at the house as Heloise had expected he would.

'If Heloise was ashamed of me, he would certainly be shocked at my appearance,' Gilda thought.

She decided that, rude or not, she would write to Lady Neyland and a maid could read it to her.

It would certainly come as a terrible shock.

She walked across the room to pull the curtains so as to leave Heloise in the dark.

As she did so, she took one last look at her sister, thinking it was cruel that she should die and leave behind everything that had been so important to her.

She was beautiful, she was a success, and if she had not married the Marquis she would have had the chance of marrying another rich man.

"How could she die at this particular moment and in such a stupid way?" Gilda asked herself.

She was quite sure that Heloise had not meant to die.

She had just taken more laudanum, not anticipating for a moment the tragic effect it would have upon her.

'Mama would have been dreadfully upset,' Gilda thought, but now Heloise was with her mother and father and they were all together.

"I am the only one of the family left," she said aloud, "and perhaps, as I am likely to die of starvation, it will not be long before I join them!"

It was a bitter-sweet thought, and once again she turned to draw the curtains.

Then suddenly an idea came to her!

It was so sensational, so explosive, that she could only stand still, staring out the window with unseeing eyes.

She asked herself how she could even consider such a thing.

And yet, the idea was there and it persisted.

Then insidiously, as in one of her clairvoyant moments, the conviction came that it was something she could do, although it was hard to believe she would be successful.

"No, it is mad! Crazy! Impossible!" Gilda exclaimed.

And yet still she could feel her brain working, turning the idea over and over, looking at it from every angle, and at the same time being convinced with a perception that could not be denied that it was something which was possible.

"However outrageous it seems, it would be better than staying here and starving," she told herself.

After what seemed a long time, she turned from the window and walked to the mirror.

She sat down as Heloise had done on the stool to look at her reflection.

As she had taken the pins out of her hair this morning it had fallen into little curls round her forehead, resembling the way her sister had looked yesterday.

Now it seemed as if the face beneath the curls were not her own but that of Heloise, and she knew there was and always had been a remarkable likeness between them, just as they both resembled their mother.

Gilda looked at herself and went on looking.

The shape of her face was the same as her sister's and so was her small, straight nose.

If anything her eyes were a little larger, or perhaps Heloise had been tired when she arrived and her eyes were not shining as brightly as they might have done.

On the dressing-table in front of her was the lip-salve which Heloise used, the hare's foot with which she added a little colour to her cheeks, and the powder which made her skin even whiter than it was naturally.

As if she moved in a dream, Gilda applied the cosmetics she had watched her sister use on her face.

After luncheon on the Saturday of her arrival, Heloise had gone upstairs to her bedroom to change from her travelling-gown into something cooler and lighter. She had sat down at the dressing-table and exclaimed:

"Heavens! I look dreadful!"

It was then that she had added the faint pink blush to her pale cheeks, made her lips glow with lip-salve, and added a dusting of white powder which Gilda had thought made her look different and in a way older than she did without it.

"Does everybody in London use cosmetics?" she had asked.

"Of course they do!" Heloise replied. "I would feel naked without them."

"It makes you look strange, but at the same time very beautiful," Gilda had said.

As she spoke she had seen the reflection of her own face above Heloise's in the mirror and thought she looked dull in contrast and rather washed out.

Now the cosmetics seemed to transform her not into a more vivid image of herself but into Heloise.

"I am the duplicate of Heloise!" Gilda told herself as she rose from the stool.

"How can I think of doing anything like this?" she asked herself, half-expecting her sister to sit up in bed and denounce her for such presumption.

But Heloise lay very still, while the sunshine touched the gold of her hair and somehow made it seem like a halo.

"I am sure she would have been kind to me if she had lived," Gilda said defensively. But she knew that was not true.

Then as if she forced herself to obey an impulse that was stronger than her own will, she went to the wardrobe.

Half-an-hour later Gilda pulled Heloise's packed trunk from the room to the top of the stairs.

Then she went back to pick up her bonnet, gloves, and reticule.

She then pulled back the curtains and went to stand beside the bed.

For a moment she looked down at her sister in the dim light before she went down on her knees.

Then she prayed fervently that Heloise might find peace and happiness and that she herself would be forgiven if what she was doing was a sin.

"If only you could tell me, Mama," she said to her mother, "that what I am about to do is wrong or right, it would be much easier for me. But I swear on everything I hold holy that if I do this, I will try to be kind and helpful and understanding to everybody I meet!"

She sighed and went on:

"There are not many people I can help here, but perhaps in London there will be those who will need my comfort as so many people needed yours. Help me, Mama, to be like you. And forgive me if you disapprove of what I am doing now."

When she had finished her prayer, Gilda wiped the tears from her eyes, then bent forward to kiss Heloise's cold cheek.

"Good-bye dearest," she whispered, "and may God keep you safe."

Then picking up the things she had laid down as she prayed, Gilda went from the bedroom, closing the door quietly behind her.

# Chapter Three

As the carriage neared Curzon Street, moving slowly through the traffic, Gilda began to panic.

'Perhaps,' she thought, 'the best thing I can do is to tell Lady Neyland that I came to London to tell her of Heloise's death and, having nothing to wear, was obliged to borrow her clothes.'

Then the same pride which had made her refuse her sister's money told her she was being ridiculous.

To go back and struggle to live on potatoes and vegetables from the garden would be to admit defeat before she had even entered the battle.

She tried to convince herself that this was an opportunity which had appeared unexpectedly to save her, and she would be not only foolish but extremely cowardly if she let it pass her by.

Before she had left the Manor she had tried

to think of everything which could allay suspicions regarding "her" death.

When she had reached the Hall she had gone upstairs again to remove the bottle of laudanum from her sister's side.

She had then thrown it away into the bushes where it was never likely to be discovered, before she went into the small Study to sit down at her father's desk to wonder how she could make things easier for Mrs. Hewlett.

Returning from her niece's wedding, she would find, as she thought, that her young mistress had died in a room she did not habitually use.

But there was no-one to whom she could turn for advice, except to send five miles for the Doctor.

"She must have some money," Gilda told herself.

It was then that she looked into Heloise's reticule which she had brought downstairs with her bonnet and gloves.

To her surprise, she found quite a considerable sum of money inside it, far more than she would have expected a lady would require if she went to the country for two nights.

She then supposed that she was being naïve and ignorant and the golden guineas were what people in London considered an ordinary amount to carry with them.

Anyway, it solved her problem, and she put the book in which she had written down her expenses on the desk as if she had been working out her accounts before she went to bed.

Then she put a sum of money beside it and marked on a piece of paper in her elegant writing:

*"Mrs. Hewlett's wages for two months."*

Another pile was labelled:

*"Tithes due on the 1st May."*

The third pile was for bills owed locally, including three sovereigns which were loose in the drawer, which Gilda thought would pay for her Funeral.

It all appeared very neat, and as there was nobody who came to the house except Mrs. Hewlett, who was absolutely trustworthy, it would not be considered strange that she had left lying about what money she had.

When the carriage arrived James fetched her trunk from the top of the stairs, then he and the coachman bade her "good-morning," and Gilda drove away, unable to look back at the house where she had lived for so many years because she felt it might make her cry.

For a long time she sat thinking of Heloise and her own desperate adventure and fighting against an urge to tell the carriage to turn back.

Then as they journeyed on she became interested in the countryside, while at the same time

her brain was busy trying to remember everything Heloise had said in their conversations.

She had to prevent herself from making mis-
takes when she reached Lady Neyland's house
in Curzon Street and it was not going to be
easy.

She knew the first difficulty would be to find
her way about the house, but she recalled that
when she had asked Heloise if it was noisy at
night in London, she had replied:

"Not in Curzon Street, which is filled with
houses belonging to aristocrats, and anyway
Godmama and I both sleep in rooms which
overlook the garden at the back."

"That is one thing I must remember," Gilda
told herself.

Then there were the servants' names.

She tried to remember if her sister had mentioned them. If she had, she could not recall
them.

Fortunately, her mother had explained to her
the different appearance of senior servants in a
grand house, and during her father's last year
in the Army when he was a full General they
had employed a Butler and a footman because
they had done so much entertaining.

"Housekeepers wear black with a châtelaine
at their waists," Gilda told herself; "lady's-
maids wear black dresses without an apron, and
housemaids wear mob-caps."

Nevertheless, when the carriage finally
stopped outside the porticoed house in Curzon

Street, her heart started to beat frantically and her lips felt dry.

A footman in the same smart livery as James wore came running down the steps to open the door of the carriage.

At the front door, a man with grey hair who Gilda knew was the Butler was waiting to receive her.

"Good-morning, Miss Heloise," he said respectfully. "It's nice to see you back. Her Ladyship's waiting for you."

"Thank you," Gilda said.

She walked towards the staircase, wondering frantically how she would find Lady Neyland's bedroom.

Then when she reached the top of the stairs she saw waiting a middle-aged woman in black without an apron and knew it must be her lady's-maid.

"Good-morning," she said, wishing she knew the woman's name.

"Good-morning, Miss Heloise," the maid replied. "Her Ladyship's been waiting for your arrival. She was upset on Saturday when she found you'd gone without saying good-bye. It's not right that Her Ladyship should be upset, seeing the state of health she's in!"

The maid was scolding her exactly like a Nanny, Gilda realised, and she thought that Heloise had been quite unnecessarily inconsiderate in going away as she had.

"I am sorry," she said humbly, and thought

the maid gave her a sharp glance as if she was surprised at her reply. They walked a little way along the passage and the maid opened a high mahogany door.

"Miss Heloise's back, M'Lady!" she announced, and Gilda walked into a very attractive bedroom, the sunshine coming through the window on the far side of it.

She saw Lady Neyland sitting in an armchair with a bandage over her eyes.

This, Gilda knew, was a test which she might fail.

She was well aware that when people were blind they were more sensitive to voices than if they could see, and she only hoped that hers would sound like Heloise's and she would not immediately be denounced as an imposter.

Lady Neyland held out her hand.

"Heloise, my dear," she said. "I have been so worried about you travelling without a Chaperone or even a maid with you."

Because her voice was so kind and not in the least reproachful as the maid's had been, Gilda moved quickly across the room.

"I am sorry . . . Godmama, very, very sorry," she said, "for upsetting you. It is something I should not have done."

"Well, you are back safely," Lady Neyland said, "and I am sure Carter and James looked after you."

"They did indeed," Gilda said.

She took Lady Neyland's hand in hers and

bent forward to kiss her cheek.

"I am sorry if you missed me," she went on, "but now I will make amends by reading you all the morning newspapers."

Lady Neyland laughed.

"I will certainly appreciate that. But just take off your bonnet and cloak, then tell me how you found everything at home. I heard from the servants that was where you had gone."

Gilda thought it was stupid of Heloise not to realise that although she had tried to deceive her Godmother, she had only to ask her own servants where they had driven her.

"Everything was all right," she said, "but I am glad to be back, very, very glad."

"That is what I want you to say," Lady Neyland replied, "and your ardent admirers will be delighted that you have returned, especially the Marquis."

There was a little pause before Gilda asked, as she knew Heloise would have done:

"Was he . . . upset when I did not . . . attend his . . . dinner-party?"

"I do not know if he was upset," her Godmother replied. "He called to take you driving in the afternoon and certainly seemed surprised that you had left without informing him of your change of plan."

Lady Neyland smiled before she went on:

"I got the impression that it was the first time any woman had refused one of his invitations in such an offhand manner."

Gilda thought that Heloise had been right. Her action had surprised the Marquis, and perhaps it would, as she had hoped, make him "come up to scratch," as she had put it.

"Anyway, I expect you will see him this evening and you can make your own explanations to him."

"This evening?" Gilda questioned without thinking.

"Surely you have not forgotten that my friend the Countess of Dorset has invited you to a dinner-party she is giving before her Ball? She told us when she was here the other day that she had seated you on the Marquis's left."

"Yes . . . of course . . . I remember," Gilda said hastily.

"Run and take off your things, dear child," Lady Neyland said. "Then we must discuss what you are going to wear. I shall want you to look your very best."

"I will try," Gilda said, "but I wish you could come too."

She thought Lady Neyland was pleased as she replied:

"I too wish I could. Nevertheless, you will tell me later all about it, so that I can feel I am not missing everything by sitting here blind as an old bat!"

She tried to laugh, but there was a little throb in her voice which told Gilda how much she minded.

"Godmama," she said. "I was thinking about

you, and I remembered how Mama always said that carrots helped our eyesight and of course green vegetables also."

She saw that Lady Neyland was listening intently, and she went on:

"I was reading a book about somewhere in the East where it was very dry and dusty and the rains came only once a year."

She paused before she continued:

"I cannot remember which country it was, but in the book it said the native inhabitants had poor physiques and suffered badly with their eyesight until after the rain, when everything sprouted. Then they ate the green shoots of the plants and trees and immediately they regained their strength and especially their eyesight."

"That is very interesting!" Lady Neyland exclaimed. "I think, dearest child, you must speak to Chef and see if he can buy fresh carrots and lettuces and other green vegetables."

"You can at least try to see what they will do," Gilda said.

"I certainly will," Lady Neyland replied, "and thank you for thinking of me."

"I will go and take off my bonnet," Gilda said. "Then I will read to you."

As she walked towards the door she was wondering where her room would be.

Fortunately, Lady Neyland's maid was waiting outside the door.

She thought the woman looked a little less

disagreeable, and Gilda said quickly:

"I wonder if you would come with me to undo the back of my gown? It will not take me a minute to change, and I feel rather hot after my journey."

She took off her travelling-cape as she spoke, and almost mechanically the lady's-maid took it from her and walked down the passage in what Gilda knew must be the direction of her bedroom.

The house was not large and her bedroom in fact was only two doors away from Lady Neyland's, and when they reached it she found that her trunk had already been brought upstairs and a young housemaid was kneeling beside it, taking out her clothes.

"So you are here, Emily!" the lady's-maid said. "Miss Heloise wishes to change her gown, so you can undo the buttons for her."

She moved away and Emily got to her feet and started to unbutton Gilda's gown.

"Miss Anderson's got a monkey on her shoulder this morning," she said confidingly.

"I am afraid that I upset her," Gilda replied, glad to know the name of the lady's-maid.

"She's angry wi' me too," Emily said, "because I scorched one of the table-cloths I were a-pressin'."

Then she looked at Gilda apprehensively as if she thought she had said too much, and asked quickly:

"Which gown do you want to wear, Miss?"

"Oh, anything cool and simple," Gilda replied.

The maid went to the wardrobe and when she opened it Gilda drew in her breath.

She had never before seen such an array of wonderful gowns. They looked as if somebody had captured a rainbow.

Because she did not wish to keep Lady Neyland waiting, she changed quickly into a crisp muslin not unlike the one Heloise had worn at home, but this one had pale green ribbons instead of blue ones, and the muslin was sprigged with tiny white flowers and pale green leaves.

It was so pretty that Gilda felt it was a gown she would have worn at a smart garden-party.

But she knew that she would have to leave it to Emily to choose what she would wear normally, and after thanking the maid she hurried back to Lady Neyland's room.

The newspapers lay on a stool not far from the chair in which Her Ladyship was sitting, but when Gilda came towards her she asked:

"Tell me what you are wearing. I want to visualise you, and one of the problems of being blind is that people forget that descriptions are very important when one cannot see with one's own eyes."

"I will try to describe everything to you," Gilda replied, "and let me say that it is a lovely day, the sun is shining, and in the country the lilacs are coming into bloom and the daffodils are gold among the trees."

She went on trying to paint a picture, and when she stopped Lady Neyland said:

"You have described it beautifully, dearest. I had no idea you were so poetical."

"Now let me tell you about my gown," Gilda said quickly.

She remembered that Heloise had never shown an interest in nature.

"Talking of flowers," Lady Neyland said, "I have just remembered that Anderson tells me there are a great number of bouquets for you downstairs. I expect you will want to go see them."

"I will see them later," Gilda replied. "For the moment I would much rather talk with you."

It was obvious to Gilda that Lady Neyland was both surprised and pleased.

She described the gown in which she had travelled to London and also her impressions of the countryside she had seen on her drive.

She was still talking when Anderson came in to say:

"Your luncheon's just coming upstairs, M'Lady, and Miss Heloise's is ready for her in the Dining-Room."

"Oh, how disappointing that I cannot eat with you!" Gilda exclaimed.

There was a slight pause. Then Lady Neyland said:

"But you must remember, dearest child, you

said only a short while ago that you hated eating off trays in bedrooms."

Gilda drew in her breath. Then she gave a little laugh.

"If I said that, it must have been when I got out of bed on the wrong side," she said. "I would much rather have luncheon with you. In fact, to be truthful, I find it depressing to eat alone."

She thought of how many meals she had eaten alone since her father had died, and how when Mrs. Hewlett had gone home the house seemed so quiet and oppressive that sometimes she talked to herself.

"I would like you to eat with me," Lady Neyland said, "but I must learn to be adventurous and come downstairs to dinner."

"Why not?" Gilda replied. "It must be boring sitting here all the time, and I am sure your friends would like to join you sometimes if you did not find it too tiring."

"I am perfectly well except for my eyes," Lady Neyland replied, "but I thought it might be embarrassing if because I cannot see I am messy with my food."

As she spoke, Gilda was quite certain that Heloise had put such ideas into her head.

"I will tell you what we will do," she said. "You will ask some of your very special friends to dinner, and I will choose dishes which you do not have to cut up but can eat with a spoon. Besides, they will understand if you do not seem very hungry and talk and listen rather than eat."

Lady Neyland gave a little laugh.

"You are making it a game! At the same time, I feel better already. Oh, Heloise, do you think my eyes will ever get better so that I shall be able to see again?"

"I know they will," Gilda said positively.

As she spoke, she knew that what she was saying was true. The conviction was there in her intuition.

She told herself that she would see the Chef immediately after luncheon and speak to him about the carrots and green vegetables, and, what was more important than anything else, she must make Lady Neyland believe that she would soon be able to see again.

Anderson, with a rather sour face, went downstairs to say:

"Miss Heloise would have luncheon upstairs with Her Ladyship."

When the two trays arrived, a table was arranged for Gilda opposite Lady Neyland's, and they talked animatedly all the time that the luncheon was being served by the Butler and two footmen.

"This is fun," Gilda exclaimed, "and much, much better than having luncheon on my own."

"That is something which does not often happen to you," Lady Neyland answered. "I think you will find there is a pile of invitations waiting for you, and now we must talk about tonight."

"I have an idea!" Gilda said. "Because the Countess is such a close friend of yours, God-mama, I am going to drop her a note and suggest that you would like to come in for an hour or so after dinner. You could listen to the music and your friends could talk to you. That would be far better for your health than sitting here all alone."

Lady Neyland was very still.

"Do you really — think I could do — that?" she asked after a moment. "I would not be a bore and an — encumbrance?"

"If the Countess is a true friend, you will be nothing of the sort," Gilda said. "In fact, I am sure she would welcome you with open arms. Please, Godmama, let me send her a note and suggest it."

"I do not know — what to say," Lady Ney-land said helplessly.

"Leave it to me," Gilda said.

She wondered where she should write the note, then felt sure that there would be a Writing-Room.

She ran down the stairs and when she reached the Hall she said to one of the footmen on duty:

"Will you look and see if there is plenty of ink in the ink-well? I have to write a letter and I want somebody to take it to the Countess of Dorset's house where I am dining this evening."

79

"Henry'll take it, Miss," the footman replied.

As Gilda expected, he went ahead of her into a room which opened off the Hall, and when she followed him she saw that it was obviously a Study which would have been used by Lady Neyland's husband when he was alive.

There was a huge mahogany bookcase filled with books, which Gilda glanced at with delight, and a large flat-topped desk with elegant gilt handles and feet and on which were a blotter and a number of white quill-pens ready to be used.

The footman looked at the ink-well and said:

"There's plenty of ink there, Miss."

"That is all right then," Gilda replied, and sat down at the desk.

She wrote quickly, hoping she was addressing the Countess respectfully enough as she suggested that it would give her Godmother so much pleasure if she could come for a short while after dinner and listen to the music and meet some of her friends.

She wrote:

Her Ladyship is in good Health, except for the Affliction in her Eyes, but I feel sure with Care and Faith her Sight will soon be Returned to Her.

She signed the letter when she had finished, addressed it, then gave it to the footman who was waiting in the Hall.

Then as she was about to go back upstairs, another footman opened the front door.

As he did so, a man came into the house and as Gilda looked at him she knew who he was without being told.

She had imagined, from the description Heloise had given of the Marquis, that he would be tall and good-looking, but she had not expected him to be so handsome and so overwhelmingly magnificent that he took her breath away.

She knew that because she had seen very few gentlemen since she grew up, any man she met in London would look different from those she had encountered in the country.

At the same time, she was quite certain that the Marquis would be outstanding wherever he was.

As he walked towards her she felt as if he overwhelmed her and for the moment she could not speak and it was also impossible to think.

"So you are back!" he said, and his voice was sharp. "I want an explanation, Heloise, of where you have been and why you should have behaved in such an unaccountable manner."

Gilda thought frantically of what she could reply, but somehow she could only stare at the Marquis, fearing that as his dark eyes searched her face, he had already penetrated her disguise.

Then she told herself that there was no

reason to think he might be suspicious, and, lifting her chin in a way that she felt Heloise might have done, she said:

"If I have inconvenienced Your Lordship I must of course apologise."

"You certainly must," the Marquis said grimly, "and perhaps we should discuss this where we can be alone."

He did not wait for her to agree but walked towards another door in the Hall, which Gilda felt must lead into the Drawing-Room.

She followed him and found that she was not mistaken.

She saw a very attractive room with a large crystal chandelier hanging from the ceiling and elegant gold-framed French furniture uphol-stered in blue brocade.

She thought it might have been chosen as a background for Heloise, then remembered that it would also frame herself.

The Marquis closed the door behind him. Then he walked in a purposeful manner to stand with his back to the mantelpiece.

Feeling a little shy, Gilda went to a sofa not far from where he was standing and sat down on the edge of it.

She knew it was foolish, but she felt like a School-girl who had been caught out playing truant, and she told herself that as he had not proposed to her sister, he had no right to be-have as if he owned her.

At the same time, because he was so overpowering she felt her heart fluttering unpleasantly and found it hard to look at him.

There was silence until the Marquis said:

"I am waiting!"

"For what?"

"You know that you have behaved unpredictably, if nothing else," he replied. "I am not in the habit of giving dinner-parties for young women who do not turn up and have not even the good manners to send their excuses."

"I am . . . sorry," Gilda said, feeling there was nothing else she could say.

"That is not at all an explanation."

"I am sorry to have upset you," Gilda said, "and most of all to have upset Godmama. I can only say I am very . . . contrite and it will not . . . happen again."

She was not looking at the Marquis as she spoke, but she had the feeling that he was staring at her in a way which she felt was intimidating.

Then he said:

"You surprise me, Heloise, and I suppose it is best if we say nothing more about this escapade. At the same time, I was extremely angry at having my plans disrupted at the last moment."

"I can understand that," Gilda said, "and it was, I admit, extremely rude of me. So I can only repeat that I am very sorry if I inconvenienced you."

The Marquis did not speak, and she managed to steal a glance at him.

She thought he was the most handsome man she had ever seen.

At the same time, there was something about the squareness of his chin and perhaps the strong line of his lips which told her that he could be not only difficult but perhaps also at times cruel.

Gilda did not believe that Heloise would have been happy with him, however much he could have given her in the way of worldly advantages.

"We will forget it," he said magnanimously.

Gilda rose to her feet.

"I know you will excuse me, My Lord," she said, "if I go back upstairs to be with my God-mother. She, too, was upset that I ran away in that foolish manner, but now that I am back I am trying to forget my misdeeds, and I am arranging for her to come to the party this evening."

"To the Dorsets'?" the Marquis enquired. "But surely as she is blind that will be impossible?"

"Why should it be?" Gilda asked. "She is not ill in any other way. It is just that her eyes are affected, and I can imagine nothing more depressing than sitting at home night after night and thinking of her friends having a lovely time while she cannot join them."

"And what do you intend to do about it?" the Marquis asked.

"I have just sent a note to the Countess asking if Godmother can join the party after dinner. She naturally feels embarrassed at having to eat in front of people, but she can sit and listen to the music, and I will be able to tell her what is happening, and what I forget you can describe to her."

"Me?" the Marquis questioned. "Are you expecting me to take part in this charade?"

"Why not, My Lord? It would certainly be a kindness, and I am sure she would appreciate your attention."

Unexpectedly the Marquis threw back his head and laughed.

"You are certainly full of surprises at the moment, Heloise," he said. "Never before have I been asked to be the eyes of somebody who is blind."

"There is always a first time for everything," Gilda replied, "and as there is quite a lot of preparation to be done, I hope you will excuse me."

"I came here to ask you to drive with me," the Marquis said. "My Phaeton is outside."

"It is very kind of you to think of me, My Lord," Gilda replied formally, "but perhaps another time."

He looked at her in a manner which told her without words that he was astonished that she could turn down his invitation. Then he said:

"If that is what you wish, of course I understand that your Godmother has a right to your company rather than myself! I shall see you to-night at dinner, Heloise, and naturally it is something to which I shall look forward."

He spoke with a touch of sarcasm in his voice, which made Gilda think that he was not being quite sincere.

Then it suddenly struck her that he thought her concern for her Godmother was just an act put on to impress or rather to intrigue him.

She guessed that he was intelligent and was quite sure that in consequence the wiles that had been practised on him by dozens of other women besides her sister had not gone undetected.

'He thinks I am trying to trap him,' Gilda thought to herself.

She thought it would be amusing if the Marquis knew she was not in the least interested in him as a man, but rather was a little afraid that he might be perceptive enough to realise that she was not her sister.

She wondered why on such short acquaintance she had received such a strong impression of him.

She in fact was vividly aware that he was clever, intuitive, and had a way of looking deep into the person he was with, almost as if he searched for something he did not expect to find.

There was no reason for her to know this, and yet she did, and her clairvoyant powers told her that if she was not careful, the Marquis might be a very dangerous enemy.

'The best thing I can do,' she thought, 'is to keep away from him as much as possible.'

Without waiting for him to say any more, she walked towards the door.

When she reached it she looked back and saw that he had not moved from the fireplace, perhaps thinking she was merely putting on an act and actually had no intention of leaving.

She dropped him a little curtsey.

"Good-day, My Lord, and thank you for your invitation to go driving. I shall of course look forward to meeting Your Lordship again this evening."

She could not help just a touch of mockery in her voice, which echoed the note she had heard in his.

Then, because actually she was shy and a little afraid, she pulled open the door.

She ran through the Hall and up the stairs before there was any sign of his leaving the Drawing-Room.


"Now tell me exactly what you are wearing," Lady Neyland said as Gilda came into her room before leaving for the dinner-party.

"I feel very beautiful," Gilda replied with a little laugh, "and that is not conceited, for it is all due to my gown, to the hairdresser, and of course to Anderson's help in making my face prettier than it really is."

As she spoke, Gilda was amused to see Anderson look quite proud.

The maid had in fact been surprised when Gilda had asked her help in using the cosmetics that she knew her sister had always applied to her face.

It was after the hairdresser had left, having arranged her hair in a fashionable style that was both becoming and elegant, that she had gone to Lady Neyland's room to ask her help.

She had chosen her words with care.

"I think, Godmama," she said, "from something somebody said the other night, that I am using too much powder and perhaps also too much rouge. I wonder if you would allow me to borrow Anderson to help me? I notice how lovely your skin looks, and that is how I would wish mine to be."

Anderson was gratified, and she certainly had a skilful and experienced touch that Gilda herself did not possess.

"The trouble with young people," Anderson said, "is that they always think they know better than anybody else. I've always wanted to tell you, Miss Heloise, that you were using too much rouge and the wrong colour. Your powder should be applied so sparingly that it is virtually invisible unless somebody looks closely."

"I am sure you are right," Gilda answered. "I will watch very carefully to see what you do."

She knew when Anderson was finished that the maid had only very gently accentuated the natural colour in her cheeks and on her lips, and the colour of her skin seemed almost natural, except that there was no shine on her small nose or her pointed little chin.

Anderson had thoroughly approved Gilda's suggestion that Her Ladyship should attend the party.

"What she wants is taking out of herself," she said. "Moping about here all the time with no-one to talk to is not the way for her to get well again."

"I agree with you," Gilda replied.

"Her Ladyship has always liked parties and being with her friends, and I can't think now why we never thought of her going to one before. She can listen and talk, even if she can't see."

"Yes, of course, and she shall not be left behind in the future," Gilda said. "I will write to every hostess who has asked me to a party and say that my Godmother must come too."

"It's kind of you to think of it, Miss Heloise," Anderson said.

She spoke in a way that made Gilda feel uncomfortably that she was thinking how self-centred she had been in the past.

But she did not wish to compare what she was doing with what Heloise had done.

She had no wish to face the fact that her sister was so selfish that it would never have crossed her mind to think of anybody else's pleasure but her own.

'I must make up for my deception by trying to give happiness to everyone with whom I come in contact,' Gilda thought, and she knew that was the only way she could make retribution for the lie she was acting.

When she thanked Anderson for attending to her face and told her how clever she was, the maid had quite a flush on her pale cheeks, and Gilda thought that the almost open antagonism she had encountered when she arrived was now forgotten.

She spent a long time choosing first which gown she should wear, and secondly which gown would be most becoming to Lady Neyland.

She too had a wardrobe filled with beautiful dresses, most of them in soft shades of mauve or grey, which Gilda heard she had worn ever since her husband had died.

"As soon as you can see again," she said, "I am going to make you buy a gown to celebrate, which will be as brilliant as the sunshine and as gay as the flowers in the window-boxes."

Lady Neyland laughed.

"If you want me to look like a bird-of-Paradise," she said, "when I am able to see for myself, we will go to the most expensive and best dressmaker in Bond Street and you too shall have some new gowns."

"I shall never be able to wear all those I have already!" Gilda expostulated.

"Of course you will!" Lady Neyland replied. "And then you will tell me you have nothing to wear! No woman ever has enough clothes."

They both laughed, but Gilda wished she could tell Lady Neyland how much the gown she was wearing meant to her personally.

After the dresses she had grown out of and which had faded and shrunk in the wash, it was like being transformed from a chrysalis into a butterfly.

Her gown was made of a gauze which was so delicate that she felt it revealed rather than concealed her figure, and it was trimmed with silver ribbons which made her think of the moonlight.

She had silver slippers to match, and a little wreath of leaves studded with diamanté which encircled the knot of curls which the *Coiffeur* had arranged at the back of her head.

"I look like a Greek goddess," she said to Lady Neyland when she described her appearance, "or perhaps Diana the Huntress, and I should be carrying a spear in my hand."

"You have already speared enough hearts as it is," Lady Neyland replied with a smile, "but we have talked so much about my gown that you have not yet told me what the Marquis said to you."

"He was both surprised and angry at my behaviour."

"I hope you apologised properly," Lady Neyland admonished. "I find him charming, but he is very conscious of his own consequence."

"That describes him exactly!" Gilda exclaimed. "I also think he is a little intimidating."

There was a pause before Lady Neyland said:

"As I have told you before, dearest, I think you are flying too high in wishing to catch the Marquis. After all, Sir Humphrey Grange is just as wealthy, if not of such great importance."

Gilda noted the name and knew that he was the other suitor for Heloise's hand, who she had said was not important enough.

"There are plenty of men in the world," she said lightly, "and quite frankly, Godmama, I am in no hurry to be married."

She spoke impulsively and knew that Lady Neyland was astonished.

"But, dearest child, you have been so insistent that you must be married! I told you over and over again that there is no hurry, as I love having you with me! You have time to think, and you must be very careful to choose the right husband to ensure your future happiness."

"Yes, I know you said that, Godmama, and you are quite right," Gilda replied, "and so I shall refuse everybody who asks me for at least another year."

Lady Neyland clapped her hands together.

"That is what I want to hear and it gives me great pleasure. Oh, Heloise, I have been so afraid that you would rush into marriage and then be as desperately unhappy as I was."

"Were you?" Gilda asked curiously. "How very sad!"

"I do not talk about it," Lady Neyland said. "My husband had many other — interests besides me, and after our marriage he really had no use for me, except as a hostess for his more — respectable friends."

Gilda understood what her Godmother implied, and she reached out to take Lady Neyland's hand in hers.

"I am sorry, so very sorry for you," she said. "It must have been very hurtful."

"What I minded more than anything else," Lady Neyland said in a low voice, "was that in consequence we had no children. I would love to have had a dozen sons and daughters to look after and to plan for as they grew older."

Gilda bent forward to kiss her cheek.

"Now you can plan for me and make sure that I do not marry the Marquis of Staverton or Sir Humphrey, but wait until somebody as charming as Papa comes along. Then I know I shall be happy, even if I have to live in a small house in the country with very little money."

Gilda spoke dreamily, thinking of her mother and how happy she had been. Then she realised that Lady Neyland, still holding her hand, had not spoken.

After what seemed quite a long pause she said:

"You have changed, Heloise, changed in a

way that is difficult to describe. I have never heard you say such things before, and certainly you have never thought of me until now."

Gilda realised she had made a mistake, but there was no turning back.

"If I have changed," she said, "it is because when I went away from you I realised how terribly kind you have been to me and how selfish I was in thinking only about myself and not about you."

Her voice rose a little as she went on:

"Now everything is changed, and we are going to do things together. If a hostess will not have you at her party, then I shall stay at home and we will gossip like two old spinsters!"

She had intended to make Lady Neyland laugh, and she succeeded.

"You are being ridiculous, child," she said, "but I love you for it. Now hurry or you will be late for the dinner-party, and do not forget, I shall be arriving at nine o'clock, and I will be feeling like a débutante going to her first Ball."

"I will be your Chaperone," Gilda said, "and see that the most eligible men sit beside you whispering sweet nothings into your ears."

Lady Neyland laughed again.

Then as Anderson put a velvet wrap trimmed with marabou round her shoulders, Gilda went downstairs feeling that it was a good thing that no-one guessed she was in fact making her début tonight in the first evening-gown she had ever worn.

She was going to the first dinner-party she had ever attended and would be dancing at her first Ball.

It was all like a dream!

As she reached the Hall she saw the carriage waiting outside to take her to the Countess of Dorset's house, and she only hoped that she would not wake up too soon and it would last at least until midnight.

# Chapter Four

Gilda lay in that delicious state between sleeping and waking, thinking how happy she was.

Last night had been a revelation and had in fact exceeded all her wildest anticipations.

She had always dreamt of seeing a Ball-Room filled with beautiful women and handsome men dancing under the glittering light of crystal chandeliers, with a Band playing softly and the atmosphere fragrant with the scent of flowers.

The dinner-party too at the Countess of Dorset's had been an enchantment.

They had sat down fifty to dinner, and the large table stretching down the middle of the room was a magnificent sight with its gold ornaments, huge golden candelabra, and decorated with orchids.

Gilda had sat staring about her wide-eyed until she realised that the Marquis was watching her and remembered that she was supposed to have been familiar with such scenes of beauty for the last two years.

Nevertheless, as the candles glittered on their hostess's enormous tiara, which was almost like a crown, she could not help murmuring more to herself than to her dinner-companion:

"This is just like a fairy-tale!"

"Why especially tonight?" the Marquis asked with what she thought was a bored note in his voice.

"Perhaps it seems more glamorous than usual," Gilda said quickly, "because I am feeling happy."

"Why?" he persisted.

"Does one have to have a reason for happiness?"

"If a woman says she is happy, it usually means that she is in love!"

Gilda laughed.

"Then I am the exception. I am happy because everything is so beautiful and everybody is so kind to me."

"In what particular way?"

She thought his questions were rather tiresome and she evaded them by turning to talk to the gentleman on her other side, who plied her with compliments.

She felt that they came too easily to his lips to be sincere, but at the same time they gave her confidence.

She was determined not to get involved in private conversation with the Marquis, and when Lady Neyland arrived it was easy to avoid it.

She caused quite a stir when she came into the Drawing-Room on her host's arm, looking, Gilda thought, very elegant in a beautiful mauve gown with a tiara on her head and a huge necklace of amethysts and diamonds round her neck.

Gilda had been clever enough to suggest before she left that Lady Neyland not wear the eye-bandage she usually wore on the Doctor's orders, but instead should substitute for it a piece of the same material as her gown.

Anderson had made up Her Ladyship's face skilfully, and with amethyst and diamond earrings hanging from her ears it was easy to forget that she looked any different from any other attractive Dowager in the Ball-Room.

The Earl of Dorset led her to a comfortable chair that had been specially arranged for her on a small dais. When Gilda joined her Godmother, she said:

"This is all due to you, dearest child, and I am so excited at hearing the music and the voices of my friends."

Her last remark gave Gilda an idea of how she could overcome a difficulty that had been worrying her all day.

She was well aware that many of the people who would wish to speak to her Godmother must have been known to Heloise for some time, and it was therefore perfectly obvious that

98

she would be expected to say:

"Here is Lady 'X' or Lord 'Y,' " as they approached.

Instead, she said:

"Now, Godmama, let us see if you recognise the voices of your friends."

Lady Neyland was only too eager to enter into the game, and nine times out of ten she guessed right the first time.

When the Marquis approached, Gilda was sure that he intended to talk to her, and she said quickly:

"Here is the Marquis of Staverton, and he has promised, Godmama, to describe to you how some of your favourite people are looking, although I am afraid he may be critical of them!"

Lady Neyland laughed.

So the Marquis, after he had kissed her hand, could do nothing but sit down beside her, which gave Gilda a chance to slip away and dance with some of the many young men who were begging her to do so.

As each dance ended she returned to her Godmother's side, but she soon found that she was not needed, for as Lady Neyland's friends circled round her she was holding Court and, as Gilda well knew, enjoying every moment of it.

Gilda had just finished dancing with the young man who had been on her left at dinner when a large, rather florid-looking man came up to her and said:

"How could you be so cruel and so unkind, Heloise, as to disappear without telling me where you were going?"

Gilda was tense, wondering who he could be, but fortunately her partner interrupted:

"You are bumping and boring, Sir Humphrey, which is something you dare not do on the race-course. Miss Wyngate is my partner until the next dance starts."

"I am not going to apologise," Sir Humphrey replied, "because I have something very important to say to Miss Wyngate and you must therefore forgive me if I take her away from you."

He did not wait for an answer but drew Gilda by the arm onto a balcony outside the Ball-Room.

Although she had no wish to go with him, she had little choice in the matter.

Fortunately, once they were on the balcony she saw that there were a number of other couples who had come out to enjoy the coolness of the evening air, and the only way Sir Humphrey could be intimate was to lower his voice.

"You are driving me crazy!" he said. "When do you intend to give me an answer? I am tired of waiting."

Gilda thought he must be referring to the fact that he had offered to marry her, and after a moment she answered hesitatingly:

"It is . . . not a . . . thing one can . . . decide in a hurry."

"Hurry!" Sir Humphrey exclaimed. "I have been down on my knees to you for over six months!"

Gilda did not speak, and after a moment he said:

"I hoped that you would encourage me by wearing my sapphires tonight. After all, although your Godmother is here, she is unable to see them."

Gilda had no answer to this, as she did not know what he was talking about. Instead she said:

"I think I must go back to Godmama. I am sure she would like to talk to you. It is very exciting for her to come here this evening after being shut up in the house for so long."

"I am not concerned with your Godmother but with you," Sir Humphrey said, and Gilda thought that he came a little nearer to her.

There was something about him that she did not like, although she thought that perhaps her feelings were unreasonable.

She did not know why, but she did not trust him and she could understand her sister's reluctance to marry him.

'If he were as rich as Midas I would not marry him,' Gilda thought.

As two more people came from the Ball-Room onto the balcony she said quickly:

"I must go and see that Godmama is all right," and escaped before Sir Humphrey could do anything to prevent her.

However, he was hovering in the background all evening, and Gilda found that she was trying to avoid not only the Marquis but also him.

At the same time, her first Ball was everything she had expected it to be.

There was no doubt that Heloise's beauty had made her a success, and even the most blasé Beaux and those who, Gilda suspected, usually stood about looking bored and contemptuous paid her compliments and obviously thought it smart to be in her company.

Going home with Lady Neyland, she thought again how terribly sad it was that Heloise should have died at the very zenith of her success.

Unimportant as far as the *Beau Monde* was concerned, she had managed to make an impression on the most critical Society in the whole of Europe.

Almost as if she was following her thoughts, Lady Neyland said:

"You were greatly admired tonight, dearest child, and I was very proud. Also, I want to thank you too for being so kind to me."

"I should be thanking you," Gilda said quickly. "If I had not such a beautiful gown and were not your Goddaughter, I feel nobody would pay any attention to me."

"Nonsense!" Lady Neyland said. "Your face is your fortune, as the saying goes, and all the gentlemen who talked to me tonight were quite lyrical in their praise of you, including the Marquis!"

"I think he is still astonished that I should have run away from him," Gilda remarked.

"I am sure he is," Lady Neyland said. "At the same time, dearest, I do not think he would make you a very good husband. The Countess was telling me that she is sure he has never been in love with anybody in his whole life."

Gilda thought that probably was true, as Lady Neyland went on:

"I cannot help feeling that he is pursuing you primarily to annoy all your other admirers and show them that he can beat them not only on the race-course but in the Ball-Room."

"You are right!" Gilda exclaimed. "And let me assure you, Godmama, I do not take him seriously."

"I am so glad, dearest, for I was so afraid that he might break your heart as he has broken so many other women's."

"He will not do that," Gilda said confidently.

When they arrived home and Lady Neyland was telling Anderson what a wonderful evening it had been, Gilda kissed her Godmother good-night, thanked her again, and went to bed.

Because she was so unused to dancing and staying up late, she had fallen asleep almost immediately.

Now she could look back in retrospect and the only thing that puzzled her was Sir Humphrey's reference to his sapphires.

What sapphires? And if he had given them to Heloise, though she could hardly believe that was true, then where were they?

Emily came in a little later with her breakfast, and Gilda found that by the time she had finished it, half the morning had gone.

"I must get up," she said to Emily.

"There's no hurry, Miss," Emily replied. "Her Ladyship's still asleep. But there's bouquets of flowers downstairs and I've some notes which came with them."

She put them down in front of Gilda on the bed, and when she opened the first she saw that it was from Sir Humphrey, and he had written:

I must see You, Enchanting Seductress. Will You drive with Me this afternoon, or may I call on You at about four o'clock?

Gilda realised that she had no wish to accept either suggestion, then almost laughed at herself to think how exciting such an invitation would have been if she were still at the Manor House.

There was no note from the Marquis, and in the majority of the *billets-doux* she had difficulty in identifying the writers.

When finally she was dressed, she said to Emily tentatively, feeling her way:

"This gown really needs a small brooch in the front."

"You are quite right, Miss," the maid said.

"Why not wear that pretty pearl one which you told me belonged to your mother?"

Gilda was still.

She knew quite well that all her mother's jewellery had been sold by her father when he wanted money to invest in his dubious stocks and shares.

When she did manage to reply, she said:

"Yes, of course. That is a good idea. Where is it?"

"In your jewel-case, Miss," Emily replied.

Gilda thought it would be a mistake to ask where that was, but Emily went to the wardrobe and opened it.

Gilda saw to her astonishment that on the floor beneath her gowns was a box made of leather, which looked like a jewel-case and appeared large enough to contain the Crown Jewels.

Suppressing her astonishment, she said vaguely:

"Now, where did I put the key?"

"I wasn't prying, Miss," Emily said quickly, "as you told me never to interfere, but I happened to notice 'twas in your reticule last night, the way you always take it with you."

"Yes, of course," Gilda answered. "I am tired this morning and feeling rather stupid."

Emily fetched the pretty satin reticule trimmed with lace that she had carried by its ribbons over her arm and which she had thought contained only her handkerchief.

But when she pulled it open she found that at

the bottom beneath the handkerchief there was a small key.

As she drew it out, to her surprise Emily said:

"I'll wait outside, Miss, 'til you calls me," and went from the room.

Gilda thought this was obviously the way Heloise had instructed Emily to behave, so she said nothing, but as soon as the door shut behind the maid she went to the wardrobe and knelt down to open the jewel-case.

It was certainly very large, and she could only suppose that Lady Neyland had given it to Heloise as a present, or perhaps it had been one of her own for which she had no further use.

She turned the small key in the lock and raised the lid.

Then she stared in sheer astonishment, for on the tray which lay inside on the top of the case there was a remarkably large amount of jewellery.

"How can Heloise have owned all this?" Gilda asked herself.

There was the pearl brooch which Emily thought had belonged to her mother but which Gilda had never seen before, and there were pearl earrings to match it and a very pretty gold bracelet set with diamonds and pearls.

In another velvet pocket there were two earrings of sapphires and diamonds and a pendant to match them.

She knew these were what Sir Humphrey

must have been referring to last night, and she was horrified that her sister had accepted such an expensive gift from a man whom she had not promised to marry and apparently had no wish to do so.

"I must send them back," she told herself.

There was also on the tray a small string of pearls which she had the uncomfortable feeling might be real.

Then she lifted up the tray and drew in her breath.

She could hardly believe that what she was seeing was not a mirage.

In the bottom of the jewel-case there were dozens and dozens of gold sovereigns!

She stared at them, feeling that what she was seeing could not be true, but if it was — where on earth could Heloise have obtained so much money?

There must, she calculated, be at least fifty sovereigns lying there.

Then it flashed through her mind that perhaps Lady Neyland was generous in giving Heloise money for tips or small purchases, and therefore there was nothing very peculiar in the fact that she had saved the money rather than spent it.

Then she saw that there was a small pile of papers amongst the gold, and she picked up the first one and opened it.

The top of the paper was headed *"Coutts Bank"* and Gilda read

Dear Madam:

We have the honour to inform you that your Deposit Account now stands at £1,959. 10s.

We wish to express our deep appreciation of your continuing custom, and remain, Madam, your humble and obedient servants.

Coutts.

Gilda thought there must be some mistake. Then she saw that her sister's name, *Miss Heloise Wyngate,* was written there at the top of the letter.

"I cannot believe it!" she said beneath her breath. "How can Heloise have accumulated so much money?"

She could not help thinking of her sister's reluctance to offer her twenty pounds a year and the conditions attached to it.

Then, as if she was afraid of what she had learnt, she put the paper back into the jewel-case, replaced the tray, and locked the box.

Then she walked over to the dressing-table to sit down on the stool and stare at her reflection in the mirror. But she did not see her own face, only that of Heloise, and heard the questions that she kept asking herself over and over again in her mind.

What did it mean? Where had this money come from?

After what seemed a long time she suddenly remembered that Emily was waiting outside. She crossed the room and opened the door to say:

"I am going to Her Ladyship's room."

"Did you find your brooch, Miss?" Emily enquired.

"I have changed my mind," Gilda replied, and her voice was somehow hard. "I have no wish to wear any jewellery."

The Marquis of Staverton, having ridden in the Park before his contemporaries were awake, came back in a good humour for breakfast at his house in Berkeley Square.

The new stallion which he had purchased the previous week at Tattersall's had given him an even better ride than he had anticipated when he bought it.

He decided that when he went to the country he would take the horse with him and try him over some fences he had erected as a miniature steeple-chase course.

He found this an excellent way to train his horses not only for racing but also for hunting.

As he settled down to enjoy one of the well-cooked dishes which his Chef had provided, his Butler said respectfully:

"Excuse me, M'Lord, but there's a messenger from the Foreign Office asking if you'll call on Lord Hawkesbury at your earliest convenience."

The Marquis looked at the clock on the mantelpiece.

"Ask the messenger to inform His Lordship that I will be with him at eleven o'clock."

"Very good, M'Lord."

The Marquis finished his breakfast, then went into his Library, where his secretary was waiting with a large pile of invitations besides a number of letters from the Agents on his Estates, asking for his instructions regarding various improvements, renovations, or alterations which had to be done.

The Marquis worked for an hour-and-a-half before the pile of correspondence on his desk had diminished considerably, then he went upstairs to change his clothes.

Looking as usual resplendent without being in the least dandified, he set off for the Foreign Office, driving a high-perch Phaeton with an expertise that was the envy of every passerby who watched him as he drove into Piccadilly, then down St. James's Street.

At the Foreign Office there was a Senior Clerk waiting to conduct him to the Foreign Secretary's Office, and as soon as he entered the room Lord Hawkesbury rose to his feet, holding out his hand in welcome.

"It was good of you to come at such short notice, Staverton," he said.

"I was naturally curious as to why you needed me so urgently, My Lord," the Marquis said.

He sat down in a comfortable armchair on the opposite side of the desk, and as the Foreign Secretary seated himself there was a worried expression on his face.

There was silence for a moment. Then Lord Hawkesbury said:

"Quite frankly, Staverton, you are my last hope."

The Marquis raised his eye-brows but did not speak, and Lord Hawkesbury said almost as if the words burst from him:

"You will hardly believe it, but I am convinced, although I have little proof of it, that there is a leak of information going out from this Office!"

This was certainly surprising, and the Marquis sat upright.

"From this Office?" he repeated. "How can you be sure?"

"I am not sure, and that is the trouble," Lord Hawkesbury replied, "and I admit that to a certain extent I am guessing. At the same time, I am desperately afraid that secret information is being carried from Whitehall to Bonaparte in some devious manner."

There was silence, and the Marquis was thinking that while the Treaty of Amiens, which had been signed a month ago, had delighted the world, Ministers like Lord Hawkesbury had been suspicious that Napoleon Bonaparte was just playing for time and was consolidating his forces.

If this was true, then in a very short while hostilities between England and France would recommence.

However, it would be useless to say such

things to the Prime Minister.

Henry Addington, who had succeeded William Pitt after his resignation the preceding year, had proved himself to be weak, vacillating, and complacent to a degree which the Leaders of the Armed Forces thought extremely dangerous.

The Marquis had on various occasions in the past been of service to the Ministry of Foreign Affairs and Lord Hawkesbury in particular, and now he was sure that if the latter was suspicious, he had grounds for it.

"What can I do about a leak if there is one?" the Marquis enquired.

"That is what I am asking you!" Lord Hawkesbury said with a faint smile.

"Explain the position," the Marquis said.

The Foreign Secretary lowered his voice as if he thought the room might have ears.

"I have investigated and had under observation, secretly of course, every member of my staff."

"And you have a suspect?"

"It is slanderous to say so, because I cannot find anything specific against him," Lord Hawkesbury answered, "and yet my instinct tells me that Rearsby is not all he appears to be."

The Marquis frowned for a moment.

Then he remembered Lord Rearsby, a rather overdressed young man whom he had seen at parties and on race-courses but had never wished to make his acquaintance.

He was not the type, the Marquis thought, that one would suspect of being dangerous in any way. He merely hung round the rich and the famous and was the sort of man who would belong to a good Club because it would advance him socially.

"Do you know him?" asked Lord Hawkesbury, who had been watching the Marquis's face.

"By sight," the Marquis replied. "He is not a man who interests me either as a friend or as an acquaintance."

"That is what I thought," Lord Hawkesbury said. "His father was the first Peer, and Rearsby went to a good School. He has a small Estate in Sussex, where he spends little time, and he is, I am told, ambitious to be recognised by the Prince of Wales."

The Marquis gave a little laugh.

"That might apply to quite a number of men."

"Exactly!" Lord Hawkesbury replied. "That is what makes me think I must be 'barking up the wrong tree.' At the same time, there seems to be nobody else."

"Why is he working here at all?"

"He came here during his father's lifetime because Lord Rearsby, who received his title as a reward for distinguished work for us, was eager for his son to follow in his footsteps."

There was a pause before he went on:

"When his father died, everybody expected young Rearsby to resign immediately and spend the money he had been left on riotous living. But strangely enough he remained, and as he is really quite conscientious in his work, there is no reason at all why we should not continue to employ him."

"And what makes you suspicious?"

"Quite frankly, I do not know," Lord Hawkesbury said. "It is just that there seems to be nobody else whom I would not trust implicitly, and also there is no-one else who has been here very much longer than Rearsby, although that has little to do with it."

"It certainly sounds very difficult," the Marquis said. "What do you expect of me?"

Lord Hawkesbury laughed.

"Again, I do not know. I am having Rearsby watched, but he has not been seen in contact with any of those whom we suspect of being sympathisers or supporters of our enemies. If he does in fact pass on any information, I cannot think to whom he gives it."

"And what can I do?" the Marquis asked again.

"Just keep your eyes open, Staverton. You have been so lucky in the past, or shall I say so astute, and as I have already said, you are my last hope."

"Is there any information within Rearsby's knowledge which could be of great advantage to the French?"

"Anything they learnt about our Army or Navy would be helpful to Bonaparte, who I am quite certain is intending to invade this island sooner or later."

"You really believe that?" the Marquis asked. "I thought it was just a weapon with which to scare old ladies and the 'fuddy-duddies' in the Cabinet."

The Foreign Secretary shook his head.

"No, I am completely serious. My information is that the French are building barges in which to convey enough troops across the Channel to attack us when we are quite unprepared for it."

"Quite unprepared?" the Marquis ejaculated. "Then why the devil are we disbanding the Navy and the Army with such unprecedented haste?"

"You must ask the Prime Minister that question," Lord Hawkesbury replied. "All I can say is that I have protested vigorously at two Cabinet Meetings, only to be overruled as usual by those who think that if they believe in peace strongly enough, their wishes will come true."

"It is crazy!" the Marquis said sharply.

"I agree with you," Lord Hawkesbury replied, "but nobody is going to listen to me unless we can prove, and I am very anxious to do so, that Napoleon has spies who keep him well informed about everything in England, so that he will strike at a moment when, because we are so defenceless, he is bound through sheer numbers to be victorious."

"That is something we must prevent!" the Marquis said fervently.

"Amen!" the Foreign Secretary replied.

The two men sat talking together for over an hour, and when the Marquis left the Foreign Office he was looking serious.

As he drove home he was doubting whether even with his proverbial good luck he would be able to find what he knew was a "needle in a haystack."

He went to luncheon at White's because he thought he would see Lord Rearsby there, and he was not mistaken.

The first Lord Rearsby had been a member of the Club, and his son had been put down for membership when he was still quite young.

There was no doubt, the Marquis thought cynically, that Rearsby found it a "happy hunting ground" in which he could further his ambitions.

There was no other Club where he could meet socially the *crème de la crème* of Society, and where as members men put aside their prejudices against one another, and a member was accepted at his face value.

The Marquis noticed that Lord Rearsby was sitting with some friends who were not important and was neither eating nor drinking to excess.

It seemed almost absurd to suspect that he was a spy for Napoleon.

At the same time, if he really had ambitions to be a great social success, he would need more money than the amount that the Foreign Secretary suspected he had been left by his father.

It was well known in the Foreign Office that Napoleon was extremely generous to those who furnished him with the information he required, and the smugglers who carried spies back and forth across the Channel found such a cargo far more lucrative than the usual ones of brandy and tea.

Immediately hostilities had ceased, there had been the usual witch-hunt for those who had been disposed to sympathise with the French, and there were endless tales of spies listening in at Cabinet Meetings or even hiding in corners at Buckingham Palace.

The Marquis had not believed any of it. He knew only too well that patriotism could blow up something very trivial into a menace from which people shrank in terror.

What was more, without the excitement of battle, women particularly enjoyed tales of intrigue and conspiracy.

Without appearing to do so, he watched Rearsby for some time, and decided that Lord Hawkesbury was mistaken.

How would it be possible for an unimportant young man to get in touch with Napoleon's spiders'-web of espionage in the first place?

If Hawkesbury had had him followed, he would surely have been detected at some moment or other in contact with those émigrés now living in London who were always suspected of trying by any means, fair or foul, to return to their native land.

"I am sure the whole thing is just imagination," the Marquis told himself.

At the same time, having worked with Lord Hawkesbury for some years, he knew that he was conscientious, level-headed, and noted for being meticulous in separating the grain from the chaff.

Because the Marquis could find nothing of interest at White's, he decided that he would call on Heloise.

He was finding her behaviour so strange that it made him curious.

He was used to women trying to be different from one another and attempting to arouse his interest by being original, and he thought he knew all the tricks they used and all the bait they threw so carefully under his nose in an effort to catch him.

But Heloise Wyngate for the moment had him completely puzzled.

He had at first been extremely angry when she had upset the numbers at his dinner-party and had not even paid him the courtesy of letting him know that she was leaving London.

If there was one thing he really disliked, it

was bad manners, either in a man or a woman, and he told himself that as far as she was concerned he was finished with her.

Then he laughed and decided it was just another carefully conceived plan to trap him into finding her irresistible.

He told himself he was far too old and too clever to be caught in such a way.

All the same, she was in fact the most beautiful girl he had ever seen, and he knew that if one of her other admirers swept her away when it was thought that he was still interested, it would definitely be a feather in his cap.

He had therefore decided that he would call and try to find out what she was doing, although he was quite certain he knew.

He was well aware how skilfully she had managed not to have any intimate conversation with him last night and had appeared to be enjoying herself with a child-like excitement which was different from anything he had noticed in her before.

When she left London, he had known perfectly well that Heloise had been concentrating fervently on him to the exclusion of everybody else in any Ball-Room or anywhere else they might be.

But last night she had been as elusive as a piece of quicksilver, and he had the strange idea, although he could not account for it in any way, that when their eyes had met there was a touch of fear in hers.

"I am imagining it," he told himself.

But the idea persisted, and he was convinced that he was not mistaken.

It had been Lord Hawkesbury who had first become aware that beneath the Marquis's Corinthian surface there was an astute, ultra-critical, highly perceptive brain.

He had therefore cultivated the young Marquis's friendship until he was in a position to ask his help in various problems which originated in the Foreign Office but overflowed into the Social World and came within the Marquis's orbit.

Because he had been so remarkably successful, Lord Hawkesbury had not only congratulated himself on discerning the Marquis's ability, but he had also begun to admire him more and more and also to rely on him.

He was quite certain that if anybody could solve the problem of what he suspected was a major leak in his department, it would be Staverton.

When the Marquis agreed to try, Lord Hawkesbury had sighed with relief, as if he had transferred a burden from his shoulders to those of a younger man.

The same intelligence and the same probing mind which the Marquis was prepared to exercise in finding Napoleon's spy, he was now concentrating on Heloise Wyngate.

He wanted to know why she had appeared to be so frightened.

Gilda worried over the contents of her sister's jewel-case until it was difficult to think about anything else.

When Anderson had insisted that after such a late night Lady Neyland should lie down after luncheon, Gilda had gone to the Study to read.

She had found a dozen books which she thought would be extremely interesting, but when she curled up in the window-seat with one of them, she found the pages dancing in front of her eyes.

Instead, she could see only the letter from Coutts Bank addressed to her sister and the pile of glittering sovereigns at the bottom of the jewel-box.

She was wondering for the hundredth time what could be the explanation, when the door opened and the Butler announced:

"The Marquis of Staverton, Miss!"

Gilda started and her book fell from her lap onto the floor.

She would have risen to pick it up, but the Marquis crossed the room swiftly and gave it back into her hands.

As he did so, he looked down at the title and saw that the author of it was Rousseau.

"You read French?" he asked.

"Quite well, and this is a book I have always wanted to read," Gilda replied.

"Why?"

"I thought it would be interesting. Both Papa

and Mama enjoyed his works, although Papa really preferred books about soldiering."

"I did not know you were a reader," the Marquis remarked.

Too late, Gilda remembered that Heloise had never read a book if she could possibly avoid it and was in fact extremely bad at French.

She only hoped that the Marquis did not know such facts about her sister, and she said quickly:

"Godmama was not expecting you to call this afternoon."

"As you are well aware, I am calling on you," the Marquis said.

"For any particular reason?"

"Do I have to have a reason?" he asked. "I thought, although perhaps I was mistaken, that we were such good friends that we liked being in each other's company."

There was that mocking note in his voice which Gilda had learnt to expect, and after a moment she said:

"I have a feeling, My Lord, that you are laughing at me!"

"Why should I do that?"

"I do not know, but perhaps it is because I have always heard you find young girls boring."

She had not heard this, but she felt certain that that would be the Marquis's attitude about most unmarried women.

"You are quite right," he answered, "but you

can hardly put yourself in the category of 'young girls,' who are invariably gauche, unfledged, and extremely ignorant."

Gilda gave a little laugh.

"You are very unkind about them. They do their best, and remember, girls grow up and become beautiful and witty women."

"Sometimes!" the Marquis agreed enigmatically. "But you are very beautiful, Heloise, and you cannot imagine to what state you have reduced the male population of St. James's."

Gilda laughed again.

"You are too skilful with your compliments. I have a feeling that either you have uttered them so often that you have become word-perfect, or else you think them out in your bath."

"Now I think you are insulting me!" the Marquis said, but he was smiling.

Gilda looked at the clock over the mantelpiece.

"I think Godmama will soon have finished her rest, and I have to change my gown."

The Marquis's eyes twinkled.

"If that is an excuse to be rid of me, it is hardly up to standard. I cannot believe, unless you had luncheon particularly early, that Her Ladyship has had time to rest, and you look so charming in the gown you are already wearing that I doubt if you will trouble to change it again."

Gilda was silent, not knowing what to say, and he went on:

"What has happened? Why are you trying to avoid me?"

"I am . . . not doing . . . that," Gilda murmured rather ineffectually.

"I am not a fool," the Marquis said. "First you run away, then when you come back you make it quite obvious that you have no wish to be alone with me. I want an explanation, Heloise, and I think I am entitled to one."

"I do not know why you should think you are . . . entitled to . . . anything," Gilda said. "You have no . . . jurisdiction over me . . . as you well . . . know."

"No?" the Marquis queried.

"No!" Gilda said firmly.

He looked at her for a long moment, and she had the feeling that his eyes were probing beneath the surface, looking deep down into her heart, and she was afraid.

Then as she struggled vainly to find a new subject of conversation, the Marquis said:

"I have an idea that we should celebrate your Godmother's return to Society by giving a dinner-party for her."

There was a sudden sparkle in Gilda's eyes.

"Do you mean that?" she asked. "It would indeed please her enormously. She enjoyed herself so much last night, but she is rather dubious this morning about my intention to write to everybody who has invited me and inform them that she must attend the parties too."

She looked at the Marquis and added:

"As you noticed last night, Her Ladyship has no wish to push herself onto anybody."

"I am aware of that," the Marquis said, "and so I will give a party for her, and you shall tell me who are her special friends whom she would like me to invite."

"May I tell Godmama of your plans?" Gilda asked.

The Marquis shook his head.

"No, I think it should be a surprise!"

"That would be even more exciting."

Gilda paused for a moment before she said:

"I had always thought that Godmama had had such an enjoyable life, until she told me how unhappy she was with her husband and how much he neglected her. I think that is why now she is very grateful for any love or kindness she receives."

Gilda spoke in a low voice, and for the moment she was thinking not of the Marquis but of Lady Neyland.

When her Godmother had talked at luncheon-time she had understood how much the attention she had received last night had meant to her.

She thought too that because Lady Neyland was still comparatively young and attractive, it must have been very depressing for her to know that Heloise was going to parties every night while she had to stay at home, just as she had done when her husband had "other interests."

The Marquis was watching the expressions that crossed Gilda's face. Then he said:

"Leave everything to me. I will arrange the party for tomorrow night."

"Are you able to do that so quickly?"

"Why not?" he asked. "We will be about twenty at dinner. I will ask about the same number of people to come in afterwards, and I expect you will want to dance."

"Not if you do not want to," Gilda said quickly. "I shall be quite happy just to sit talking or to watch your guests playing cards."

The Marquis looked at her as if he thought she could not be speaking the truth, but again she was concentrating on Lady Neyland, and after a moment she said:

"Of course cards are no use to Godmama, but she would like to hear music, even if no-one dances."

"Then we will have music," the Marquis agreed.

"And please," Gilda said quickly, "could we choose a special dinner that Godmama can eat easily?"

"I see that like me you think of every detail," the Marquis said. "I have already decided that whatever the rest of us eat, your Godmother shall have food which she can eat with a spoon."

"That is very kind of you," Gilda said, "and thank you very, very much. I am sure that nobody has given a party exclusively for her in a very long time."

"Then I shall take care to invite her special friends," the Marquis said. "And what about you? If you are still determined to avoid me, you will need your special admirers there."

Gilda thought of Sir Humphrey and gave an involuntary little shiver.

"Tomorrow evening is nothing to do with me," she said. "Please ask only those people who will amuse Godmama and of course yourself."

"You are very self-effacing all of a sudden."

To his surprise, Gilda blushed and the colour rose up her throat towards her eyes.

Then as if she felt shy she rose to her feet.

"Are you trying to be rid of me before I am ready to leave?" the Marquis enquired.

"I thought . . . perhaps you . . . would have . . . a lot to do."

"You still have not told me why you have an aversion to my company."

"It is not that . . . I promise it is not . . . that!" Gilda said without thinking.

"Then what is it?"

She searched for words but could not find them, and after a moment she said unhappily:

"I do not . . . like having to . . . answer questions."

"I am curious," the Marquis said. "I find it annoying when people are unpredictable and I cannot discover a reason for it."

Then as if Gilda was amused that he was puzzled she gave a little laugh.

"I had the feeling before you said that," she said, "that you could solve any problem that presented itself to you."

The Marquis was startled by her reply because it seemed almost as if it might have some connection with what Lord Hawkesbury had said to him, and as if she were somehow reading a message.

Suddenly he had the feeling, although it was a vague one, that when there had been French words or phrases introduced into the conversation in the past, Heloise had not understood them.

It was considered smart — a fashion set by the Regent — to intersperse one's own language with smatterings of the languages of other nations.

The Regent often spoke in French or in Italian, and the Marquis was proficient in both languages, but there were few women of his acquaintance who could do the same.

To test Heloise he quoted the French adage which, roughly translated into English, meant:

"A little learning can be dangerous for little minds."

There was a quick laugh before she replied in extremely good French:

"Now you are really being insulting, and I

think, *Monsieur le Marquis,* you are insinuating that I was boasting when I said I enjoyed Rousseau."

There was no doubt that she could speak French very well indeed, and the Marquis said:

"Ten out of ten! And may I apologise for doubting you?"

"That is something you should certainly do," Gilda replied. "And perhaps I should ask why you are so good at French, unless of course you are an admirer of Napoleon?"

"I am told that all the ladies who visit Paris," the Marquis said, "find him a most impressive figure. In fact, those who have recently returned from there go into eulogies over the manner in which the First Consul received them and the pomp and grandeur they found at the Tuileries Palace."

Gilda did not speak, and after a moment the Marquis said:

"Perhaps you would like to visit Paris with your Godmother when she is in better health?"

"Certainly not!" Gilda said so sharply that her voice seemed to ring out. "I think Bonaparte is a monster! And the sufferings he has inflicted in all the countries of Europe should ensure that no decent person would ever speak to him again."

The Marquis was astonished.

He had found few women interested in the war except for the fact that it deprived them of the silks and ribbons they required for their gowns.

If they thought of the conflict at all, it was the shortage of eligible males for social occasions which annoyed them, rather than the suffering of those who became involved in the war.

"I have seen some of the men recently discharged from the Army and Navy," Gilda went on in a low voice, "coming home without legs or arms, crippled for the rest of their lives. It is cruel . . . it is horrible for human beings to inflict such . . . injuries on one another . . . and so many of those who die are very young and have not really begun to live before they are buried."

The Marquis was stunned into silence, and the tears were in Gilda's eyes as she said:

"It is not only the soldiers who suffer in battle. Papa told me how horses scream when they are wounded and often are left to bleed slowly to death. They do not know what is happening . . . and how can they . . . understand why they should be . . . slaughtered for no . . . apparent reason?"

Now the tears ran down her cheeks, and as if she could not bear him to see her weakness she brushed them quickly away with the back of her hand.

Then she said hastily before the Marquis could speak:

"I must go to Godmama. Thank you . . . My Lord, for your . . . kindness in giving . . . a party for her . . . and please tell me if there is . . . anything I can do to . . . help."

Her words seemed to fall over one another,

and without looking at the Marquis she went quickly from the room, leaving him staring after her in sheer astonishment.

# Chapter Five

The Marquis returned home after a luncheon-party which had been of particular interest to him because all the guests except himself were politicians, and they had talked of the situation between France and England in a frank manner which he had found extremely informative.

As he went to the Library he was followed by his secretary with a list in his hand.

"What is it, Carrington?" the Marquis enquired.

"I thought you would like to see the names of the guests who have accepted for your party this evening, My Lord," Mr. Carrington said. "I am afraid there will be rather more than you first intended."

"I anticipated that," the Marquis said as if to himself.

He was well aware that when he sent out invitations there were very few people in the *Beau Monde* who would refuse, and although he had planned his party for Lady Neyland at the last moment, everybody to whom he had spoken about it had accepted with delight.

He took the list from his secretary and glanced down it, thinking that he had been clever in choosing both men and women who he knew would interest Lady Neyland, while there were also a number of younger men who would want to meet Heloise.

The Marquis thought he was being rather magnanimous in arranging that she would be admired and flattered as usual.

At the same time, he had a reason for it.

Because Heloise's behaviour towards him had surprised him so considerably during the last few days, he wanted to see her behaviour with the other men who he knew were paying her court.

In the past he had thought that while she was making it obvious that she wished to be with him, she was deliberately flirtatious and provocative with the rest in order to make him realise how much she was admired.

He was, however, aware that at the Ball the other night she had not appeared to be in the least flirtatious but had talked quietly and sensibly with her partners, and as far as he could ascertain, she had appeared to hurry away from those who were too ardent.

"Why has she changed?" he asked himself. "Or is this a new way of making me interested that has not been tried before?"

He thought he knew every move of the game and that every approach, however subtle, had been made to him before until he could almost sense exactly what would happen next.

But Heloise was now surprising him, and why she continued to run away from him when they might be together left him baffled for an explanation.

Mr. Carrington broke in on his reverie as he said:

"At the moment, with those who are coming in after dinner, your guests total sixty, My Lord."

"I think we can accommodate them," the Marquis said with a smile.

He looked down at the list once more. Then he said:

"Add Lord Rearsby to the list and send a groom with the invitation right away."

Mr. Carrington thought for a moment. Then he said:

"As Lord Rearsby has never been invited before, My Lord, I am afraid I do not know his address."

"White's Club," the Marquis said, and turned to the letters on his desk which were waiting to be signed.

He knew that Rearsby and quite a number of his friends would be very surprised at his invitation, but he thought he owed it to Lord Hawkesbury to have a closer look at the man who he suspected might be a spy.

'Not that I am likely to learn anything on so short an acquaintance,' the Marquis thought. 'At the same time, what else can I do?'

He knew he was not likely to meet Lord Rearsby at any of the parties given by his intimate friends, and because of his own reputation of being extremely fastidious in choosing those with whom he associated, he had deliberately avoided making his acquaintance in White's.

What was more, to do so would undoubtedly make those who knew him well question his reasons for approaching Rearsby, and if the young man was in fact involved in espionage, it would put him on his guard.

"No," the Marquis said to himself. "If he is here tonight it will merely be assumed that he has come with a party of some of my other friends, and nobody will think it strange."

There were other letters waiting for him, but he picked up the list which Mr. Carrington had left beside him on the desk and read it again.

It struck him that Heloise had not contributed any of the names to the party he was giving for her Godmother, and he thought it might be a good idea to consult her again as to whether there was any particular friend of Lady Neyland's who should be included.

He also, although he would not admit it to himself, was anxious to see Heloise again, and last night after he had gone to bed he had found himself quite unexpectedly puzzling over her behaviour towards him.

It was only a short distance from the Marquis's house to Curzon Street, but as his Phaeton was outside he stepped into it without thinking, drove himself round the Square, and a few minutes later had drawn up outside Lady Neyland's house.

He noticed that there was another Phaeton being walked up the street to keep the horses from becoming restless and wondered if it was somebody calling on Heloise.

The front door of Lady Neyland's house was open, and as he walked in there was only one footman on duty, who hurried to take his hat and riding-gloves.

"Is Miss Wyngate at home?" the Marquis enquired.

"She's in the Drawing-Room, My Lord," the footman replied.

"Do not bother to announce me," the Marquis said, and walked across the Hall to the Drawing-Room.

As he put his hand on the handle he heard Heloise scream.

Gilda had awakened that morning with a feeling that tonight would be very exciting because it would please her Godmother.

At the same time, she knew it would also be exciting for her because she wanted to see the Marquis's house and, if she was honest, to see him again.

Despite the fact that he frightened her, especially when he asked probing questions which made her afraid that he might guess at her deception, she found him very different from the other men whom she had met since she came to London.

It was difficult to explain even to herself exactly what that entailed.

She supposed it was because the Marquis was so much more intelligent than the young men who paid her fulsome compliments or talked in bored, blasé voices because it was the fashion.

'It would be very interesting to be friends with him,' she thought to herself, but she knew that such a thing was impossible.

She was perceptive enough to realise that he must have been aware that her sister was pursuing him, and she had the suspicion that he had known that Heloise's precipitate departure for the country was a ruse to bring him to the point of proposing marriage.

Gilda was quite certain in her mind that this was something the Marquis had no intention of doing, and certainly not to an obscure young woman called "Heloise Wyngate," who had no other attributes to recommend her except her beauty.

Her mother had always said that the great aristocrats of England invariably had arranged marriages because it benefitted their families either with money or with land.

"Anyway," Mrs. Wyngate had gone on, "those of blue blood, like Royalty, are allied with their equals, and although I hope, dearest, that you and Heloise will both make advantageous marriages from a social point of view, what is more important than anything else is for you to be in love with the man you marry."

Her voice had softened as she had said:

"Your father had no reason to marry me except that he loved me, and I not only loved but admired him so tremendously that I never thought I would be fortunate enough to become his wife."

Gilda had thought then that the one thing she wanted was to marry for love.

But as she had looked round the Ball-Room at the Countess of Dorset's, she had thought that however glamorous the guests looked, quite a number of them did not appear to be particularly happy.

At the same time, this was the Marquis's life, though it was not hers, and if she was honest it was not Heloise's either.

"Perhaps in the end," she told herself, "Heloise would have had to marry Sir Humphrey."

Then she shuddered at the mere idea of it, knowing that for some reason she could not explain, he made, in Mrs. Hewlett's words, "her flesh creep."

When Lady Neyland had gone to lie down

after luncheon, having protested that there was no reason for it and that she was not tired, Gilda had gone to the Drawing-Room to arrange some flowers that had arrived for her that morning.

They consisted of bunches of tulips and daffodils, and as she put them into a big crystal rose-bowl she thought it strange that Society spent most of the summer in London when the country was so attractive.

"If I were the Queen," she said to herself, "I would arrange to be in London during the winter, where it would be much warmer, and spend the summer months in the country, where the flowers are blooming, the sun is shining, and it is lovely to be out-of-doors."

Then she remembered that if she were at home at the moment, she would not be enjoying the flowers but working hard in the vegetable-garden.

Digging often made her hands hard with occasional blisters on her palms, and she had been afraid at first that somebody might notice that her hands were not as soft or as white as Heloise's.

But as a result of having nothing strenuous to do they were becoming softer, and she thought now that few people would guess how vigorously she had had to dig and hoe to have enough vegetables to eat.

"I am so very, very lucky to be here," she told herself, and she was humming a little tune

when the door opened and a footman announced:

"Sir Humphrey Grange has called, Miss."

Gilda gave a little start and was just about to
say that she was not at home, when suddenly
she had an idea.

"Show Sir Humphrey in, Henry," she said,
"but give me a minute to go upstairs and tidy
myself."

As she spoke she slipped across the room and
left the Drawing-Room by another door which
took her through an Ante-Room and out into a
passage where she climbed the back stairs to
the First Floor.

She ran to her bedroom, opened the jewel-
case, and took out the sapphire earrings and
pendant.

She wrapped them in a piece of tissue-paper,
and without bothering even to look in the
mirror and tidy her hair she ran downstairs
again.

She had decided during the night that she
had no intention of keeping the present that Sir
Humphrey had given to Heloise.

She knew that until she had returned the sapphires she would always feel more uncomfortable in his presence than she did anyway and
would also find it difficult to rid herself of his
attentions while ostensibly she was under an
obligation to him.

When she returned to the Drawing-Room,
entering by the same door as she had left it, Sir

Humphrey was standing by the mantelpiece, looking even more florid and flamboyant than he had at the Dorsets' Ball.

"Good-afternoon, my fair enchantress!" he said as Gilda advanced towards him.

She held out her hand and to her consternation he raised it to his lips, not in the perfunctory manner that was customary but kissing it passionately in a manner which made her shudder.

His lips were warm and possessive, and when he tried to turn her hand over so that he could kiss the palm, she snatched it away from him.

"I adore you!" he said. "Your beauty blinds me, and I hope today you will be a little kinder than you were the other night."

"I have something for you, Sir Humphrey," Gilda said in what she hoped was a quiet, calm, but firm voice.

"What is that?" he enquired.

"It was . . . kind of you to give me those . . . fine sapphires," Gilda began, "but I should have . . . explained when I . . . received them that I cannot accept such a . . . valuable gift. It would not be right."

"Now what do you mean by that?" Sir Humphrey enquired.

He spoke aggressively, and although Gilda felt nervous she stood her ground.

"Please . . . understand," she said, "that I appreciate your . . . thoughts of me . . . but you know as well as I do that it is . . . wrong for a

. . . lady to accept . . . any gift . . . except perhaps flowers . . . from a man who is not . . .
connected with her in . . . any way."

She stammered over the words because she
could not quite think of how she should put it,
and Sir Humphrey said:

"That is easily remedied. I have asked you to
marry me. I am waiting for you to say 'yes.' "

Gilda drew in her breath.

"The answer . . . Sir Humphrey, is 'no'!"

He stared at her and now she felt as if his
eyes had a most ferocious expression in them.

"What do you mean 'no'?" he snapped. "You
have played me along very skilfully until now,
with: 'perhaps,' 'someday,' 'sometime.' What
has occurred that you should suddenly shut me
out?"

"It . . . is not . . . that," Gilda said hesitatingly.

"Of course it is!" he answered. "Are you
telling me that Staverton has popped the question? The betting at White's was fifty-to-one
against him doing so."

"No . . . no . . ." Gilda said quickly. "It is just
that I have no . . . wish to be . . . married at the
moment . . . and please . . . Sir Humphrey . . .
take back your present."

She held out the sapphires as she spoke, but
Sir Humphrey made no effort to take them
from her.

"Something has happened," he said. "Something has changed you. You made it quite ob-

vious until now that I was at least the second string to your bow."

Gilda thought that he was more intelligent than she had given him credit for. At the same time, she knew it would be dangerous if he became too inquisitive.

"It is only . . . to tell you," she said, "as I have told my Godmother, that I am . . . happy to stay with her for at least . . . another year before being . . . married to . . . anybody, and she is very pleased with my . . . decision."

"Stuff and nonsense!" Sir Humphrey ejaculated. "I do not believe a word of it! You have some reason for getting rid of me, and I want to know what it is."

"It is . . . not like . . . that," Gilda said unhappily.

"Then what is it?" he demanded.

He stood looking at her. Then the aggressive expression in his eyes changed to something very different.

Gilda had no idea how lovely she looked with the sunshine coming through the windows picking out the gold in her hair, her eyes worried and a little anxious, and, because she was nervous, her lips trembling.

"I love you!" Sir Humphrey said suddenly. "I love you and I will teach you to love me! Let us have no more of this nonsense, Heloise. I will deck you in diamonds and give you everything you want in life."

As he spoke he put his arms round Gilda and

pulled her roughly against him.

She was not expecting such a move and it took her by surprise.

"Please . . . please . . . !"

Sir Humphrey seemed very large and overpowering. He was also very strong, and although she struggled against him, pressing her hands against his chest to free herself, she realised that she was helpless in his arms.

"I will make you love me!" he said, and as his mouth came towards hers she knew he intended to kiss her.

She twisted her head, but she felt his lips passionate and demanding on her cheek, and as his arms tightened she knew it was only a question of time before he kissed her lips.

"No! No!" she cried.

Then, because she was frightened of the passion she felt rising within him and the insistence of his lips against her skin, she screamed.

It was not a loud scream but one of fear such as might be given by a small animal which was caught in a trap.

Then as she thought she was lost and the next second Sir Humphrey's mouth would hold hers captive, the door of the Drawing-Room opened and she heard a voice ask angrily:

"What the hell do you think you are doing?"

She knew then that she was safe, and with a cry quite different from the one she had given before, she struggled free of Sir Humphrey as he loosened his grip and ran across the room.

Without thinking what she was doing, she threw herself against the Marquis, holding on to him because for the moment he stood for everything that was secure and safe in a nightmare of terror.

He stood still just inside the door, and as Gilda hid her face against his shoulder he put one arm round her.

He was looking at Sir Humphrey, who was glowering at him ferociously like a turkey-cock that has been challenged by another.

"I asked you a question, Grange," the Marquis said, and his voice was sharp, like the crack of a whip, and icy.

"What has it got to do with you?" Sir Humphrey asked in a furious tone. "Heloise tells me you are not engaged, and I had asked her to marry me, which I understand is more than you have done!"

"Whatever I may or may not do," the Marquis returned coldly, "I do not force my attentions on a woman who is unwilling and who screams for help."

"Doubtless knowing that her Saviour was within hearing!" Sir Humphrey sneered.

He bent down and picked up the sapphires, which had fallen to the floor while they struggled. Then he said angrily:

"Very well, Miss Wyngate, I will take back my jewels and my offer of marriage. You have made it quite clear where your ambitions lie. I only hope that you will not be *disappointed*."

He accentuated the last word and walked past the Marquis and out of the room, slamming the door behind him.

For a moment it was impossible for Gilda to speak. Then she raised her head and said incoherently:

"I . . . I am . . . sorry."

The Marquis looked at her face, which he saw was very pale, and he was aware that she was still trembling although not so convulsively as when she had first reached him.

She walked away from him towards the window to stand with her back to the room, fighting for composure.

She had been terrified by Sir Humphrey in a manner which now seemed to her rather foolish.

Yet, because such an encounter had never happened to her before, she had been unable to think but could only struggle for freedom as if her very life depended on it.

As she stood trying to get her breath back, it flashed through her mind that after what Sir Humphrey had said, the Marquis would be aware that he had given her jewels, and she could imagine nothing more humiliating.

'I cannot explain,' she thought, 'and it is best to say nothing. I am sure he despises me anyway.'

The beat of her heart had almost returned to normal, and after what seemed a long time she said again in a small, hesitating little voice:

"I am . . . very sorry."

"So you should be," the Marquis said in an unfeeling tone. "If you encourage a man like that, you must expect him sooner or later to behave like a beast."

"He . . . he frightened me."

"I should have thought that by now you were used to handling men who lose their heads and their self-control under what I imagine is severe provocation."

The Marquis spoke in a cynical, sarcastic manner which Gilda thought was worse than if he had shouted at her.

Then once again she was trembling, but in a different way from before.

"Come and sit down, Heloise," the Marquis said suddenly. "I want to talk to you."

"No . . . please . . . !" Gilda protested. "There is nothing to . . . talk about. I cannot explain . . . but I only hope that Sir Humphrey . . . meant what he said . . . and will not speak to me again."

"You mean that?" the Marquis enquired.

"Of course I mean it! I thought from the first moment I saw him that he was . . . horrid, and there is . . . something about him which is very . . . unpleasant."

Only as she finished did she realise that she was speaking as herself instead of as Heloise.

It must have been obvious to the Marquis or to anybody else who knew her sister well that she had in fact encouraged Sir Humphrey as an admirer and, as Gilda now knew, the donor of expensive presents.

"I . . . cannot talk . . . about it," she said quickly. "Please . . . leave me alone!"

"I will in a moment, if that is what you really want," the Marquis answered. "In the meantime, I came here to talk to you about to-night."

Because it was a relief that he did not insist on talking any further of what had just occurred, Gilda moved slowly from the window towards him and sat down in one of the chairs near the fireplace.

As she did so, she knew that the Marquis was looking at her in that penetrating manner which she had noticed the first time she saw him.

Quite unexpectedly he said sharply:

"Look at me!"

Obediently Gilda turned her face up to his, feeling suddenly shy but at the same time unable to take her eyes from his.

"I believe you really are frightened," the Marquis said almost as if he spoke to himself.

"It is . . . very stupid of me but I . . . cannot help it."

"I will see that Grange does not worry you again," the Marquis said. "If he calls, refuse to see him. If he persists, let me know, and I will deal with him."

"I . . . I do not want to . . . put you to any . . . trouble."

"It will be no trouble," the Marquis said. "I dislike the man and always have."

He looked at her for a moment. Then he said:

"But we will not talk about him. I have brought you the list of guests I have invited to my party tonight for your Godmother, and I thought you might tell me if there is anybody you wanted me to add to it."

"Thank you. That is very . . . kind of . . . you."

She took the list which the Marquis held out to her and wondered what he would say if he knew that she had very little idea who any of the people were whose names had been neatly inscribed by Mr. Carrington.

She thought that she ought to contribute something. At the same time, for the moment she felt as if her mind was a blank and she could not even remember the name of the gentleman who had been so pleased to see her Godmother at the Countess of Dorset's Ball.

She forced herself to read the list slowly, knowing that the Marquis would expect it of her. Then she said:

"It looks perfect to me. I am sure Godmother will be thrilled to meet so many old friends."

"They really are her friends?" the Marquis asked.

"I think so."

The Marquis looked at her with a faint smile on his lips.

"You have lived here for two years," he said. "You must have some idea by now who Lady Neyland likes and who she does not."

"Of course!" Gilda said quickly. "All the people she . . . likes best are . . . included on your list."

She thought as she spoke that he must think her very insensitive and very selfish.

In fact, she was sure that he was condemning her for being so inattentive to Lady Neyland that she did not even know the names of her personal friends.

But there was nothing Gilda could do about it except to say again:

"I am sure you have thought of everybody who is . . . important."

"I gather you do not wish me to ask Sir Humphrey?" the Marquis asked.

Gilda gave a little cry of protest, then realised that he was teasing her.

"That is not . . . funny!"

"Why have you this aversion to him suddenly?" the Marquis asked. "And what did he mean by saying he had given you jewels?"

Quickly, because she was frightened, Gilda gave the only possible reply to that question.

"He . . . he offered me . . . some," she said, "but I . . . refused them."

"Curse his impertinence!" the Marquis exclaimed. "Surely he realises that you are a lady? Jewels are what one offers to . . ."

He stopped as if he felt he was being too outspoken, but Gilda guessed what he had been about to say.

She knew, because she had read about it and her father had mentioned it once inadvertently, that mistresses received jewels as well as money from the men who became their protectors.

She realised that the Marquis thought Sir Humphrey was treating her as a "fast woman" whose favours could be bought, and the idea brought the colour flooding into her face.

It was not only the embarrassment to herself, but it suddenly struck her that perhaps in some way she could not understand, Heloise had obtained the pearls, the brooch, and the other objects of jewellery in her case in such a manner.

Because she was so agitated, she rose to her feet and without really thinking what she was doing took a few steps towards the door as if she would leave the room.

"Running away from me?" the Marquis asked. "There is no reason for you to do so, Heloise, because I am about to leave."

Gilda turned towards him.

"I should . . . thank you," she said in a low voice, "for saving me and for arriving at . . . exactly the . . . right moment."

She could not help a little shiver passing through her as she thought that if he had not come when he had, Sir Humphrey would have kissed her, and she could imagine nothing more unpleasant or degrading.

"Forget it," the Marquis said sharply, "and I

have told you that if he is troublesome I will deal with him. But in future try not to incite men to indiscretion, although that appears to be a pastime in which most women indulge."

"It is certainly . . . something I have no wish to do," Gilda replied, "and I promise you it is something I would . . . never do . . . deliberately."

She thought that the Marquis looked at her again to see if she was really being truthful in what she was saying.

Then he smiled and held out his hand.

"*Au revoir,* until this evening, Heloise. We will see, if nothing else, that your Godmother enjoys herself."

"I shall enjoy it too," Gilda said, "and thank you very, very much for being so kind."

"You can thank me if it is the success I intend it to be," the Marquis replied. "You had better go and lie down now and get over the shock of what has just happened."

He spoke kindly in a way he had never spoken to her before, and Gilda replied impulsively:

"You told me to forget it, and I intend to obey you."

"That is certainly a step in the right direction," the Marquis said, "and something you have often omitted to do in the past."

She put her hand in his and he found it was very cold.

"Good-bye," he said, "and think only that

this evening is going to be, I hope, extremely amusing."

"I know it will be," Gilda said.

As he took his hand from hers, she had the feeling that she wanted to hold on to him.

She knew it gave her a feeling of safety and security and that he protected her not only from Sir Humphrey but from the fear of being discovered.

Then she told herself she was being absurd. The first person who might become aware of her deception was the Marquis, and she should in fact be more afraid of him than of anybody else.

As he reached the door he turned to smile at her once again, and she knew, however inconsequential it might be, that she was not now afraid of him.

The Marquis's house always looked very attractive by candlelight. In fact, the Prince of Wales had said to him quite angrily on one occasion:

"I have spent a fortune on Carlton House, and dammit, Staverton, I cannot achieve the same artistic effect at night that you contrive to do."

The Marquis, who had no wish for the Prince to be jealous of him, had quickly eulogised over the house that was the talk of London and the pride and joy of the Prince himself.

It was not yet finished but had already cost an astronomical amount of money, most of it in the form of debts which were unlikely to be met for a long time.

To Gilda the Marquis's marble Hall with its pink granite pillars and exquisite statuary set in lighted alcoves was so beautiful that she found it hard to move up the carved and gilded staircase which led to the First Floor.

When she had left her own wrap upstairs and that of Lady Neyland, who had said she would wait for her rather than struggle up the stairs, she had returned to the Hall and her Godmother had taken her arm.

"Where are we, dearest child?" Lady Neyland had asked.

"It is to be a surprise," Gilda answered, "and when you meet your host you must guess who he is."

A few minutes later the Marquis received them in a huge Salon lit by three enormous crystal chandeliers, and Lady Neyland exclaimed at his first word of greeting:

"I know who you are, My Lord! Are you my host for this evening?"

"I am indeed," the Marquis replied, "and may I welcome you as my Guest of Honour, for the party is given for you!"

"How wonderful!" Lady Neyland exclaimed excitedly. "I cannot believe it. How could you be so generous and so kind?"

There was no doubting the excitement in her

voice, and Gilda smiled at the Marquis and he smiled back.

With Lady Neyland on his arm, he presented to her all the other guests for dinner, and Gilda noticed that the majority of them were in fact old and dear friends.

"The Marquis has been very clever," she told herself, and thought how inadequate she had been in contributing to the guest-list.

At the same time, she thought it would be difficult for him, however critical he might be, to find fault with either her Godmother's appearance or her own.

She had ordered the *Coiffeur* early so that he could spend a great deal of time arranging Lady Neyland's tiara to its best advantage, then adding to the newest style in which he had done her own hair several white camelias which echoed the decoration of her gown.

It was such an expensive gown that she felt guilty at wearing it, almost as if she felt she must apologise to her sister for doing so.

But she knew she had made the right choice when as she described her appearance to Lady Neyland she had exclaimed:

"Oh, I am so glad you are wearing that gown tonight! When I chose it I thought it was one of the prettiest I had ever seen, but I also thought, although I may have been mistaken, that you did not care for it."

"You were very mistaken!" Gilda said quickly. "I think it is absolutely beautiful! I cannot thank you enough for giving me something in which I feel like a Fairy-Princess."

Lady Neyland laughed.

"Let us hope there is a Fairy-Prince at the party to tell you how beautiful you look."

Gilda did not reply.

She thought, although she was not sure, that the Marquis, as the party was being given for her Godmother, would invite much older men and there would be no-one to pay her the compliments which she had received the other night from her various dancing-partners.

But she was pleasantly surprised when she noted that there were several young men in the Salon who moved eagerly to her side and vied with one another in trying to keep her attention.

Strangely enough, Gilda found it difficult to listen to them, because she found her eyes straying towards the Marquis.

He was at Lady Neyland's side, putting a glass of champagne very carefully into her hand so that there was no chance of her spilling it, and making sure that the new arrivals who came after dinner were informed for whom the party was being given.

'No-one could be more kind,' Gilda thought.

She wondered, because it was something she had not suspected, whether kindness was characteristic of the Marquis or if in fact this was something which had never happened before.

At dinner Lady Neyland was on the Marquis's right, and although Gilda was much farther down the table she could not help noticing how he was explaining to her what she had to eat, and frequently he moved her plate a little nearer to her or handed her a spoon or whatever piece of cutlery she required.

'He *is* kind,' Gilda thought again, and was sure that very few men of the Marquis's standing would take so much trouble over a blind woman.

When the dinner, which had been more delicious than any other meal she had eaten, was over the ladies retired to the Drawing-Room and almost immediately afterwards people began to arrive.

It was then that Gilda saw that the room opening out of the Salon was as big, if not bigger. It had been cleared of furniture and there was a small String Band at the far end of it.

The room was beautifully decorated with flowers and there were French windows opening out onto the garden where fairy-lights edged the paths and Chinese lanterns hung from the trees.

It was only a small garden, and she was not aware that the Marquis's father had converted it from a piece of wasteland into what in the daytime was an exquisitely landscaped garden with a miniature waterfall and rock plants which had been brought from all over the world.

The garden was surrounded by a high wall so that anybody using it could do so in private, and tonight it seemed mysterious and undoubtedly very romantic.

When the Band started to play, the Marquis took Lady Neyland into the Ball-Room where some chairs had been arranged in one corner, where she could sit with her friends who could watch those who danced and describe to her the attractive gowns the ladies were wearing.

"Tell me who looks lovely," Lady Neyland asked, "apart from my Goddaughter, of course."

"She is the Belle of any Ball-Room she graces," the Marquis replied, "but I think perhaps you would admire the Princess de Lieven more than anybody else."

"Is she here?" Lady Neyland enquired. "I have always admired her, but feel I am not really grand enough for her to know."

"Then you must certainly meet her tonight," the Marquis said. "The Russian Ambassador is unfortunately not able to be present, but his wife is an old friend of mine, and I am honoured to learn that at such short notice she cancelled an important engagement in order to come here."

A little later when the music stopped he introduced Lady Neyland to the Princess and the handsome young Russian Diplomat with whom she had been dancing.

"You are full of surprises, My Lord!" the

Princess de Lieven said to the Marquis, touching his arm with her fan. "What could be a more delightful surprise than this intimate party which I find is full of my most charming friends and none of my detested enemies!"

The Marquis laughed, knowing that the Princess because she had a sharp tongue had many enemies.

When he had left her to talk to Lady Neyland, he went to greet some other newcomers, noticing as he did so that for Gilda there was no shortage of partners.

The younger men in the party vied with one another in dancing with her, then taking her into the garden.

She would not let them take her too far from the lighted windows, knowing it would be indiscreet to venture into the shadows or to sit in any of the secluded arbours she could see in the faint light from the Chinese lanterns.

"You are being very prim and proper all of a sudden, Miss Wyngate," one of her partners said to her.

Gilda's chin went up and she looked at him sharply, and after a second or two's silence he said:

"Are you shocked that I should speak in such a way?"

"Yes, I am," Gilda replied.

"Then I must apologise," he said. "But the last time we met you were very much kinder to me than you have been this evening."

This made Gilda feel uncomfortable, wondering what he meant by being "kind," and having the embarrassed feeling that perhaps this was one of the young men whom Heloise had allowed to kiss her.

Because she knew she had nothing to say, she was forced to resort to her old trick of running away.

"I must go to my Godmother," she said hastily. "I have a feeling she needs me."

She sped back through the long windows and crossed the now empty floor to Lady Neyland's side.

She was talking to a gentleman sitting next to her, and Gilda waited for a pause in the conversation before she said:

"I just came, Godmama, to see if there was anything I could bring you."

"How sweet of you, dearest," Lady Neyland said. "No, I have everything, and I cannot begin to tell you how much I am enjoying this lovely party."

"You have been keeping yourself away from us for far too long," the gentleman beside her said, "and now that you have come out of seclusion, I assure you no party will be complete without you."

Lady Neyland laughed with sheer delight and Gilda turned away, knowing that there was no need for her to worry about her Godmother.

'The person to worry about is me,' she thought. 'I wonder how many other pitfalls dug by Heloise are waiting for me to fall into?'

At the same time, she could not feel anything but elated and excited because she could dance and look attractive enough for the gentlemen to compliment her.

And also because she was in the Marquis's house, which was more impressive than any house she had ever seen before in her whole life.

She thought also as she looked across the room to where he was talking with some friends that no man could be more handsome or more majestic.

"No wonder Heloise wanted to marry him," she said to herself, and found it difficult to attend to what the young man who had just come to her side was saying.

# Chapter Six

"I find the dancing very warming," Gilda's partner said as they finished a spirited quadrille.

"So do I," she replied.

They walked towards the open window and out into the garden.

It was slightly cooler but there was no breeze, and Gilda moved towards a seat that was beneath one of the trees on which there were several Chinese lanterns.

"Can I get you a drink?" her partner enquired.

"Thank you," Gilda replied, "a glass of lemonade would be very refreshing."

He walked back towards the house, looking for a servant, and Gilda opened her reticule to take out her handkerchief.

She had found that Heloise had a small reticule to match every one of her gowns. They were only little bags made of the same material as the gown, but usually trimmed with lace and ribbons which made them very pretty.

She had just drawn out a tiny lace-trimmed handkerchief which was embroidered with her sister's initial when she heard a low whisper behind her say:

"Drop your reticule!"

For a moment she felt she could not have heard aright.

Then the whisper came again.

"Drop it, I say!"

She was so surprised that she did as she was told, pushing it off her knee.

A second later a gentleman came forward, saying in a clear voice:

"Allow me, Miss Wyngate!" and picked the reticule up from the grass on which it had fallen.

Gilda looked at him, thinking that she had never seen him before.

He was young, dark, and quite good-looking, but there was nothing particularly distinguished about him.

He handed her the reticule with what was almost a flourish, and she said automatically as she took it:

"Thank you very much!"

"It is a pleasure!" he replied.

He bowed to her with a graceful courtesy and walked away, vanishing into the crowd who were now coming from the Ball-Room in search of fresh air.

Gilda stared after him in bewilderment.

She found it difficult to believe that she had actually heard the whisper which had told her to drop her reticule to the ground.

There seemed to be no point in it.

Then as she replaced her handkerchief in the small bag she realised that there was something at the bottom of it which had not been there before.

She could feel that it was narrow and hard, but before she could investigate further her partner returned, a servant behind him carrying a silver salver on which were two glasses.

Instantly Gilda closed her reticule by pulling the ribbons tight, and placed it over her arm where it had been before while she was dancing, and accepted a glass of lemonade from the salver.

Her partner took the other glass, which was filled with champagne, and sat down beside her.

"Do I need to tell you that you are undoubtedly the most beautiful person here?" he asked. "But of course you must get bored with hearing that."

"Not really," Gilda replied, "only surprised when there are so many beautiful women present."

She thought as she spoke that she had grown quite clever at treating compliments lightly, as if she were used to them, and did not behave as might be expected of a country girl who had never received one before.

They continued their conversation for a few minutes, but Gilda could not help thinking how much more interesting it would have been if she had been talking with the Marquis.

She wondered what he was saying to the Princess de Lieven, with whom she had seen him talking before she left the Ball-Room.

The Princess was noted for her wit, and Gilda thought dismally that she would never be able to interest the Marquis in the same way.

Then she asked herself why she should be so anxious to interest him, and was afraid of the answer.

The music had started again and she rose to her feet.

"I suppose," her partner said, "it is useless to ask you if you will dance with me again?"

"Perhaps later in the evening," Gilda replied, knowing she was booked for at least the next six dances.

They went towards the house, but instead of going in through the Drawing-Room window she changed her mind and deliberately went in through a door.

A number of the guests were returning to the house that way, and Gilda was sure they were heading for the Supper-Room.

The crowd pressed in round her and she realised that her partner was no longer beside her. Suddenly she was aware of a sharp pull on the ribbons of her reticule, which was over her left arm.

She put out her free hand to draw it close to her, and as she did so the pull came again, this time sharper than it had been at first.

She looked round and saw that behind her there was a tall, rather distinguished-looking man, and felt that it could not be he who was pulling at her bag.

It was difficult to turn in such a crowd and she had only a fleeting glance of him before her right hand touched her bag, but at the same time she found to her astonishment that his hand was on it too.

She gave an exclamation of surprise, and immediately he withdrew his hand, saying as he did so: *"Pardon."*

Then he seemed to be swallowed up in the crowd.

Gilda moved forward and a moment later was back in the magnificent Hall with the staircase in front of her.

She hurried up it and went to the room where she had left her and her Godmother's wraps when they had arrived before dinner.

The bed was now piled with elegant cloaks, shawls, furs, and stoles.

There was a maid in attendance who curtseyed when she entered, and there was a lady sitting at the dressing-table.

Gilda passed through the bedroom into another, smaller room where there were also cloaks on the bed, but here there was no maid in attendance.

She went to the wash-hand-stand and, with her back to the open door behind her, opened her reticule.

She knew it was impossible to go on dancing without satisfying her curiosity as to what the strange gentleman who had whispered to her had placed inside.

She drew out first her handkerchief, then beneath it she saw a very small roll which appeared to be made of writing-paper.

She looked at it, wondering what it could possibly be, and it struck her that it might be a love-letter written to Heloise by the gentleman who had placed it there, but he was of course unknown to Gilda.

The small roll, little thicker than one of Gilda's fingers, was sealed with a wafer such as was used on letters.

Carefully she removed it and undid what was, as she suspected, just a piece of writing-paper.

It was inscribed in such minute lettering that she found it difficult to read what was written. Then as she held it in the candlelight she managed to decipher the words:

*H. M. S.* Dreadnought *has been laid up.*
*H.M.S.* Endeavour *in dock.*
*H. M. S.* Invincible *leaves for the West Indies on May 15th.*

Gilda stared in astonishment at what she had read. Then there was a space and she read on:

*Two Battalions of King's Dragoon Guards*
*move to Dover on May 11th.*
*One Battalion of Dragoon Guards at*
*present on manoeuvres at Folkestone.*

Gilda looked curiously at what was written.

Suddenly an idea came to her which was so horrifying that she felt the small piece of paper tremble in her hand.

There was another message a little farther down but she did not stop to read it.

Instead she rolled the paper back as it had been before and pressed the wafer into place.

Then she wondered frantically what she should do.

She heard voices in the next room and quickly replaced the tiny roll in her reticule.

As she did so, she realised that there was another piece of paper flat on the bottom of the bag, which she had not touched before.

She pulled it out and opened it, and then she saw, incredibly and unbelievably, that it was a note for one hundred pounds!

For a moment it was impossible to breathe!

Then as she crinkled the note and pushed it back into her reticule she knew why her sister had so much money in her jewel-box and what the paper she had just read meant.

She remembered how her father used to tell

her of spies who carried information to the enemy and who were always a menace to any Commander who wanted to move his troops into position without being detected.

It was apparently an operation at which her father had excelled, and he also had had what seemed to be almost a "sixth sense" in his ability to detect amongst his own men those who were traitors and who were prepared to accept bribes.

"I flatter myself," the General had said, "that I have never made a mistake and have never punished an innocent man unfairly."

At the same time, Gilda realised what harm could be done and how many lives lost if the enemy was aware of the strength of the forces against them and where they were being deployed.

When the Armistice had come, even among those living in the country there had been some who said they did not trust Napoleon's overtures of friendship and were quite certain he was "up to no good."

Gilda did not have to be very perceptive to guess that what had been put in her reticule was in fact information for the French.

That her sister had been a messenger between the man who had whispered to her to drop her reticule and the other who had tried to take it from her in the crowd was horrifying.

Yet it was a clever idea, with the two men closely concerned never in contact with each other, and the only communication between them the pretty reticule of a young girl.

"How could Heloise do . . . anything so . . . abominable, so . . . wicked?" Gilda asked herself.

Then she wondered frantically what she should do now that she knew her sister's secret, and worse still, she was left in possession of the vital information.

For a moment she wished frantically that she had let the reticule drop to the ground as the man who pulled it expected, instead of holding on to it tightly.

He doubtless would have picked it up in the same courteous manner and handed it back to her and nobody would have thought there was anything strange about it.

Had he now gone away discomfitted? Or would he approach her again?

Suddenly Gilda was very frightened.

She had not listened to her father without realising how ruthless an enemy could be when it concerned important information, and downstairs he would be waiting for her.

Then she knew that whatever the dangers she ran personally, whatever terrors she might experience, they were completely unimportant beside the necessity that the secrets of the country should not pass into the hands of the enemy.

"What . . . shall I . . . do? What shall I do?" she asked herself.

Suddenly she knew the answer.

She would take the roll she had received to the Marquis.

For a moment she felt overwhelmed with relief that she had found a solution. Then she remembered it was not as easy as that.

He would undoubtedly question her closely as to how and why it should happen to her. How could she possibly tell him that the message recording the movements of British ships and Regiments was accompanied by a note for one hundred pounds?

It meant that Heloise was accepting money for taking part in espionage against England, and this, unless she was mistaken, was a criminal offence for which she could be shot as a traitor.

Gilda felt herself tremble at the thought of facing the interrogation that was inevitable if she got in touch with the Marquis.

What was more, she could give no answer to his questions without not only incriminating her sister but being forced to admit that she had deceived him and Lady Neyland by taking Heloise's place.

'I cannot do that,' she thought.

She realised frantically that time was passing. If she did not quickly take action of some sort, the Marquis might think it strange that she was not in the Ball-Room and send somebody in search of her.

"What . . . shall I do? What shall I . . . do?"

she asked herself again.

She felt there must be an answer to her problem, but she could not imagine what it could be.

The maid came into the room to look for a wrap which lay on the bed, and Gilda picking up her reticule from the wash-hand-stand walked through the other bedroom and out into the passage.

As she did so a servant came out of a door which was almost opposite, and Gilda knew by the way he was dressed that he was a Valet.

On his arm he was carrying a coat which she thought she recognised as one worn by the Marquis.

In his hand he had a pair of highly polished Hessian boots.

The man saw Gilda looking at him, and shutting the door behind him he made a respectful bow of his head and passed on down the passage.

Gilda stood still until he was out of sight.

Then looking round and seeing that there was no-one in sight, she swiftly opened the door of the room from which the Valet had just emerged and went inside.

As she had suspected, it was undoubtedly the Marquis's bedroom.

There was a large four-poster bed hung with red silk, the Staverton coat-of-arms embroidered over the head of it.

She had time for only a very quick look in the

light of the candles burning on a dressing-table.

Opening her reticule, she drew out both the roll of paper and the hundred-pound note, and hurrying swiftly to the bedside she thrust them as far as she could reach under the turned-back sheet down the middle of the bed.

Then she opened the door again and slipped back into the passage.

It had taken her only a few seconds, but as she hurried down the staircase and back into the Ball-Room she felt as if she had passed through a traumatic experience which had taken hours.

A gentleman was waiting for her and he reproached her because he thought she had forgotten their dance.

When he took her onto the dance-floor Gilda looked round for the Marquis, wondering what he would think if he knew what had happened.

He was talking to an elderly man and she longed to run to his side and tell him how frightened she was.

Supposing the man who had tried to pull the reticule off her arm was watching her?

When the dance was over she went to Lady Neyland's side.

"You are enjoying yourself, dearest?" her Godmother asked.

"It is a lovely party," Gilda said, "but I think it is time, Godmama, that you returned home. I am sure the Doctors would not approve of your being up so late, or rather I should say 'so early,' as it must be long after midnight."

Lady Neyland laughed.

"I feel as if I were a débutante and you my worried Mama!"

"That is exactly what you are!" Gilda replied with a smile. "And you must not get over-tired."

Lady Neyland protested a little half-heartedly that it was too early to leave, and Gilda's partners with whom she had promised to dance protested vehemently.

They had no idea that she was afraid to leave the safety of the Ball-Room, and although she could not see the man who had pulled at her bag in the crowd, she sensed that he was some-where near, waiting so that he could get her in a quiet place and demand what was no longer in her keeping.

She did not in fact feel safe until the Marquis had seen them into Lady Neyland's carriage and they were driven away back towards Cur-zon Street.

As Lady Neyland went into the carriage first, the Marquis asked Gilda:

"You have enjoyed yourself?"

"It has been a wonderful evening!" she re-plied.

He looked at her in the light of the flares which the linkmen were holding outside the house and asked unexpectedly:

"What is worrying you?"

He was too perceptive, Gilda thought. At the

same time, she had the feeling that he stood for safety and security in a world that was suddenly, frighteningly menacing.

She did not answer his question, and he said quickly:

"I will see you tomorrow," and helped her into the carriage.

As Gilda led her Godmother up the stairs of her house in Curzon Street, Lady Neyland said:

"I have never known the Marquis to be so kind or so considerate. I always thought he was a hard man, but now I have a very different impression."

Gilda did not speak and Lady Neyland went on:

"Lord Hawkesbury was telling me tonight how clever he is and how he admires him more than any other young man in the *Beau Ton.* That is a great compliment from the Secretary for Foreign Affairs."

Gilda drew in her breath.

"He was there tonight?" she questioned.

"Yes, of course. His Lordship was sitting beside me for a long time. You must remember him. He came to luncheon about three months ago before my eyes became bad."

"Y-yes . . . of course," Gilda said quickly.

"He gave me an impression of the Marquis quite different from what I had thought of him before," Lady Neyland went on.

They reached the landing at the top of the

stairs, and as Gilda led Lady Neyland towards her bedroom she said:

"I think I have changed my mind, dearest. Perhaps he would make you a good husband, especially if he loves you."

Gilda did not answer, and as Anderson started to take off Lady Neyland's tiara she kissed her Godmother good-night and went to her own room.

Only then did she feel as if those last words were echoing in her mind.

"If he loves you!"

She gave a little laugh that was more of a sigh.

He was never likely to do that!

She could not help feeling that it would be very, very wonderful to be loved by the Marquis, but it would be something which would never happen to her.

She knew that Heloise had wanted him because he was rich, because he had a great position in Society, and because of his vast possessions.

Thinking of him as she stood still in the centre of her bedroom, Gilda knew that none of those things mattered.

That the Marquis was a man was all that concerned her, and like a blinding light shining from the Heavens she knew that as a man she loved him.

It seemed ridiculous, absurd, something she had been quite certain would never happen, yet when as she stepped into the carriage he had said: "I will see you tomorrow," she had felt her heart turning a somersault.

The worry in her mind vanished, to be replaced with a strange excitement that came from within her breast.

He wanted to see her, and whatever other horrors might be lurking in the shadows, waiting for her, she would be able to see him.

She walked across her bedroom to sit down on the stool in front of the dressing-table as if her legs would no longer carry her.

"How can this have happened?" she asked herself. "How can I have fallen in love with somebody who is as far away from me as the moon?"

She thought she had known ever since she came to London that Heloise's aspirations where the Marquis was concerned were absurd.

He had no intention of tying himself to a young, unimportant girl, however beautiful she might be, and what was more, he was aware that Heloise, like so many other women, was trying to trap him into marriage and their transparent manoeuvres had merely amused him.

He had saved her from Sir Humphrey, he had given a party for Lady Neyland, but he had not asked her to dance.

He had in fact made no effort to talk to her except casually when they had first arrived and again when they left.

"Why could I not have fallen in love with one of the young men who were so eager to dance with me?" Gilda asked herself, and knew the answer was that the Marquis was so different from any other man.

"I am a fool!" she told herself.

Yet when she got into bed and blew out the candles, all she could see in the darkness was the Marquis's face and all she could hear was his voice when he said:

"I will see you tomorrow."

Then she thought of what was waiting for him in his bed, and told herself that he must never, never know who had placed it there.

Somehow, whatever terrors the future might hold from the men who had used Heloise as their messenger, she must not turn to the Marquis for help.

Then because even that was unimportant beside her own feelings, she hid her face in her pillow and whispered despairingly:

"I love him!"

Dawn was just coming up over the horizon and the last evening stars were fading in the sky when the Marquis said good-bye to the last of his guests.

Everybody told him it was one of the best parties they had ever attended.

"The trouble with you, Staverton," one of his friends said, "is that you do everything better than we do, even being a host."

"Thank you!" the Marquis said with a smile.

"I am complaining, not complimenting you," his friend retorted, and they both laughed.

Lord Hawkesbury had left soon after Lady Neyland and Gilda had departed.

He had not said anything intimate to the Marquis, but when he put his hand on the younger man's shoulder as they walked towards the front door, the Marquis knew that the Foreign Secretary was tired and worried and was thinking, as he had said earlier in the day, that he was his last hope.

"It has been an enchanting evening, my dear Raleigh," the Princess de Lieven said as she left.

She and the Marquis had had a brief *affaire de coeur* the previous year.

It had been a fiery encounter between two people who enjoyed each other's brains and who knew that for both of them such a liaison was just a way of passing the time with nobody being hurt in the process.

Now they were friends, and as a friend the Princess said:

"That Wyngate child is very lovely and very well behaved. I was watching her tonight, and I thought how much she has improved since I last saw her. It is strange, but she gives the impression of being much younger than she was last year."

The Marquis looked at the Princess in surprise and she laughed.

"I am perhaps being ridiculous, but my Russian instinct tells me she has changed from what she was and she might in fact be the secret jewel you are always seeking and so far have failed to find."

The Marquis merely smiled and kissed her hand, but when she had gone he thought that it was typical of the Princess with her Russian intuition to put into words what he had been thinking himself.

When at last he could go to bed he walked up the staircase thinking that his guests had been sincere, and it had, for some reason he could not quite ascertain, been one of the best parties he had ever given.

Also, there was no doubt who had been the most outstandingly beautiful person present.

He had thought when Gilda arrived before dinner that she seemed to be enveloped with a light which came from within herself, and she had no need of jewels because the candlelight shone on the gold of her hair, and her eyes, because she was excited, were like the blue of the sea.

"She is certainly very lovely," he said to himself.

As he went to his bedroom he remembered that the evening was entirely due to her because in the first place it had been her idea that Lady Neyland should attend the Ball given by the Countess of Dorset, and it was also due to

Gilda that he had suggested giving a party for Lady Neyland at his own house.

But why, he wondered, should Heloise suddenly have thought of taking her Godmother with her when there had been dozens of parties she had attended without her? And never in her conversation had she indicated that she was even aware of her Godmother's existence.

He was so puzzled that it occupied his mind the whole time his Valet was helping him undress.

Then when the man had left him the Marquis stood for a little while at the open window, watching the dawn creep up the sky and breathing in the early-morning breeze which swept away the heat of the night.

The Marquis was so strong that he did not feel particularly tired, and although he had risen early and it had been a long day, he was looking forward to his ride before breakfast.

He had taught himself when he was in the Army to sleep very little when occasion demanded, and he knew that if he had three hours now it would be enough.

Harris had blown out the light on the dressing-table and there was now only the one left beside his bed.

He closed the curtains and walked to the bed. He got in and was just about to blow out the candle when his foot struck something that felt hard.

The Marquis thought it strange and threw

back the sheet he had already pulled over him to investigate.

There, lying in the centre of the bed, he saw the little roll of paper that Gilda had put there, and beside it a crumpled note.

Sitting up and pushing aside the curtain which hung between him and the lighted candle, the Marquis investigated.

Lord Hawkesbury listened incredulously as the Marquis, who had been his first caller as soon as he arrived at the Foreign Office, related what he had found.

Then as he undid the roll of paper which the Marquis had handed him he exclaimed:

"I was right, Staverton! This information must have come directly from this Office, and it was in fact communicated to me by the First Lord of the Admiralty only yesterday."

"And the reference to the Regiments?" the Marquis asked.

"I learnt that the previous day from Lord Hobart."

"The Secretary of State for the Department of War!" the Marquis said as if he was recalling Lord Hobart's office for himself.

"Exactly!" Lord Hawkesbury said.

"It is incredible!" the Marquis said. "But, having obtained such information, why should they hand it over to me?"

"It certainly narrows the field," Lord Hawkesbury said.

"You mean it must have been somebody who was at my party?" the Marquis said.

"It makes it easier for us to eliminate them one by one," Lord Hawkesbury said.

"I have been doing that already," the Marquis replied, "and I cannot believe that there is a traitor amongst my personal friends."

"If there is a traitor," Lord Hawkesbury said, "then there is also a patriot. The person who placed this information in your bed was obviously saving it from falling into the hands of the enemy, or perhaps having a somewhat belated change of heart."

"Yes, of course," the Marquis agreed, "and I have thought that too. But it still seems clear that the information was obtained from this Office, carried by somebody unknown to my house, and placed for no possible reason I can think of in my bed, so that I should find it when I retired."

"It sounds rather like something out of a Play," Lord Hawkesbury agreed. "At the same time, you know as well as I do that it is damned serious. It brings us back to my first suspect, Rearsby, who was at your party. In fact I was very surprised to see him there."

"I invited him so that I could take a better look at him," the Marquis said. "If in fact it was Rearsby who was passing on the information, why should he then relinquish it, and to me of all people?"

"I agree there is no easy answer to that question," Lord Hawkesbury said, "but at least I am now completely convinced in my mind that Lord Rearsby is at the bottom of all this."

The Marquis was silent. Then he said:

"I am going home now to find out from my servants if they noticed anyone entering my bedroom at any time during the evening. I felt I should not question them until I had seen you."

"Quite right," Lord Hawkesbury replied. "It is important that as little as possible is said about this. At the same time, I must leave enquiries to your good sense, which has never failed us in the past."

"I must say that whatever has happened before has never been quite so strange or so unexpected," the Marquis said with a smile.

"The most important thing that you have already established, as far as I am concerned," Lord Hawkesbury said, "is that Rearsby is a thief and a traitor. But we must hold our hands and not let him be suspicious that we are on his trail until we find out who his connections are regarding this very important piece of paper."

He looked at the roll again and said angrily:

"This is just the sort of information Napoleon needs if he is to invade these shores, as he intends to do."

"At least this will not reach him," the Marquis said soothingly, and rose to his feet.

He held out his hand, saying:

"There is no need for me to emphasise, My

Lord, how important it is that Lord Rearsby should not suspect that we are on his track. If he learns from the intended recipient that this information has not been received, then he may try again, in which case we will be able to apprehend him at once and stop another spy from accomplishing the destruction of our country."

"That is Napoleon's whole aim and object," Lord Hawkesbury said sharply, "and if you and I can prove conclusively what is happening, perhaps it will wake even the Prime Minister out of his lethargy."

"We can only hope so," the Marquis agreed.

As he drove away from the Foreign Office he was wondering which of his servants he should question first, and decided that Harris, his Valet, should be the one.

Accordingly when he arrived home in Berkeley Square, he went to the Library and sent a servant for Harris.

The Valet had been with him for over ten years and he came into the room with a slightly cocky air about him which the Marquis knew meant that he was worried in case something had gone wrong.

"Your Lordship sent for me?" he asked.

"Yes, Harris. I need your help."

He realised that the man relaxed a little, but he did not speak, and the Marquis went on:

"Last night somebody went into my bedroom during the party and left a note for me. Unfortunately it was not signed, and I am anxious to know who wrote it."

"Left a note for you, M'Lord?" Harris questioned. "I never saw it."

"It was in my bed," the Marquis said.

Harris gave an exclamation of surprise.

"I'll lock the door in the future, M'Lord, when there's anyone strange in the house. It's not right that these young ladies who are always chasing you should walk in and out of the rooms as if they owned the place!"

The Marquis was amused to think how fiercely protective his Valet was of anything that concerned him personally.

"Well, it has happened," the Marquis said, "and it is embarrassing for me to receive *billets-doux* and not know who wrote them."

"That might be any number of ladies, M'Lord," Harris said.

This was an obvious impertinence and the Marquis frowned. Then there was silence before Harris said:

"I think I've got an idea as to who it was as wrote to Your Lordship."

"You have, Harris?" the Marquis enquired.

Harris nodded his head.

"I was just taking Your Lordship's things downstairs last night when I sees a lady standing in the doorway of the room opposite."

The Marquis was listening intently and the Valet was aware of it.

"Very pretty she looked, too, M'Lord. She

stops when she sees me, an' I thinks as how she looked interested in what I was holdin' on my arm."

The Marquis was well aware that Harris liked to tell a story in his own way, and to encourage him he asked the obvious question.

"What were they, Harris?"

"Your riding-coat, M'Lord, and your new pair of Hessians which I had a job to get polished right."

"And who was this lady you thought was watching you?" the Marquis asked.

"The prettiest of any of the ladies as have come to the house in the past, M'Lord," Harris said, "and they was saying downstairs last night as how there was no-one to touch her in the Ball-Room."

The Marquis waited and Harris finished:

"I'm speaking, M'Lord, of Miss Wyngate!"

"I thought you might be," the Marquis replied, "and you really think it was she who left the *billet-doux* for me to find?"

"It must have been," Harris replied, "but nobody's had the impudence 'til now to place them in Your Lordship's bed."

The Marquis frowned again.

Then after what seemed a long pause he asked:

"You noticed nobody else who might have been responsible?"

"No, M'Lord. There was nobody else about at the time, and when I leaves her she was still standing in the open door where the cloaks was left."

"Thank you, Harris, for your help. That will be all," the Marquis said sharply.

When he was alone he sat thinking of the information his Valet had given him and found it incredible.

How could Heloise Wyngate possibly be mixed up in something like this?

His frown deepened as he remembered that when she had been frightened by Sir Humphrey Grange and he had entered the Drawing-Room of Lady Neyland's house, she had run to him for protection.

When she clung to him he had felt her tremble against him convulsively and had realised how frightened she was.

And last night, when he had said good-bye to her, he had thought that she looked worried, and there may have been an expression of fear in her eyes.

The Marquis turned the idea over in his mind. Then he told himself that she had been afraid and once again had turned to him for protection.

He sat for a long time thinking it over, determined to do nothing in a hurry.

Then he knew it would be best for him to talk to Heloise when she would be expecting him, which would be immediately after luncheon when her Godmother went to lie down.

It seemed a long time to wait, but the Marquis told himself it was the sensible thing to do, though he knew it would seem to him even longer than the two or three hours involved.

But it mattered — it mattered to him tremendously — that Heloise should not be involved in what was undoubtedly a very unsavoury mess.

Thinking back, he remembered, because unconsciously he had been watching her, that she had not come back into the Ball-Room until the dance before she and Lady Neyland left was already half-finished.

He had noticed her absence because she had danced every previous dance from the beginning until the end.

He had thought how graceful she was and how very lovely in her youthful simplicity, compared to the other women in the room, who were all much older.

He had in fact invited no other young girl. Yet he knew it was not only Heloise's youth which made her stand out, but the excitement in her very expressive eyes, the smile on her lips, and the way every movement she made seemed to express a joy that came from her heart.

Then she had come back into the Ball-Room where her partner had been waiting for her for some minutes.

That must have been when, according to Harris, she was upstairs.

She had then suggested to her Godmother

that they should leave, and when he said good-night to her she had seemed worried.

It all fitted neatly into the puzzle which the Marquis was turning over in his mind, but he knew he had not unravelled the whole truth as to how or why Heloise was involved.

Where had she found the incriminating piece of paper? Or if she had been handed it unexpectedly, then why had she not brought it to him directly?

Why had she gone to the trouble, and indeed taken the somewhat reprehensible step, of going into his bedroom and slipping it under the bed-clothes?

She had known he would find it there, and she must have realised he would know the significance of its contents.

It seemed to be the act of somebody very stupid, but Heloise was not stupid.

The Marquis suddenly struck his clenched fist down hard on his desk.

"Dammit!" he said aloud. "I will get to the bottom of this!"

Then as he heard his own voice vibrate round the room, he knew he would do everything in his power to prevent Heloise from being involved.

# Chapter Seven

As they finished luncheon, Lady Neyland said:

"I admit to being tired today and am looking forward to a rest."

"We were very late," Gilda answered with a smile.

"I know, but it has done me good," Lady Neyland replied. "I feel quite different, and I am sure when the Doctor comes tomorrow he will say I can take off my bandage."

"You must not do anything too quickly," Gilda warned.

"I promise you I shall be careful," Lady Neyland replied, "and if I am able to see again, I shall be very, very grateful for my eyes."

"Mama always said we were never grateful enough for the things God gave us."

"I was thinking about your mother this morning," Lady Neyland said, "and how fond I was of her. I was also wondering if you ever hear from your sister."

Gilda was very still.

"My . . . sister?" she asked after a moment.

"You told me," Lady Neyland went on, "that she had gone to live with relatives in the far North. Surely she writes to you?"

Gilda drew in her breath.

"I have not heard from her for . . . some time," she answered.

When she had taken Lady Neyland upstairs to rest, she knew she had been hurt once again by Heloise's indifference and dislike of her.

The truth was that her sister had been afraid that Lady Neyland might want to include her in some of the parties and Balls to which she was invited and had therefore disposed of her unwanted relation by putting her out of reach.

"How could she have been so unkind after all we were to each other as children?" Gilda asked herself.

Then she knew it was no use being hurt over something which could not be remedied.

She did not want to think of Heloise's unkindness and selfishness but rather to remember how pretty she had been as a little girl when they had played together in the garden and shared their dolls.

When Gilda had left Lady Neyland in her room, she went down to the Salon knowing that once again there would be a number of flowers to arrange.

It was a task she had taken over from the housemaids, who disliked flower-arranging and said they had no time for it.

"It's most kind of you, Miss, to do it," they had said gratefully.

One of her admirers of the evening before had sent her a huge bouquet of lilies and another one of roses that were just coming into bloom.

Gilda carried the flowers into the Drawing-Room where a footman had already left two vases ready for her and filled them with water.

The sunshine was coming through the open windows, and having arranged the roses she was standing with an armful of lilies when the door opened and somebody came into the room.

She turned her head, then felt her heart leap as something came alive to vibrate through her whole body.

It was the Marquis, and because he had not been announced it was almost a shock to see him.

For a moment she could not move, and the Marquis looking at her with her hair haloed in the gold of the sun and the lilies in her arms thought she might have just stepped out of a stained-glass window.

"I thought I would find you alone at this time," he said in a deep voice.

He walked towards her and only when he reached her did Gilda manage to take her eyes from his and drop him a small curtsey.

"I must . . . thank Your Lordship for a . . . wonderful party last night . . ." she began in a hesitating little voice, wondering why it was so difficult to speak and thinking that he must hear the frantic beating of her heart.

"I want to talk to you."

She put the lilies down on the table and smoothed down her gown a little nervously as she walked towards the sofa.

She seated herself on the edge of it and looked up at the Marquis enquiringly.

It was then that she realised he was looking serious, with a slight frown between his eyes, and she wondered if he was annoyed about anything.

There was silence as if he was feeling for words. Then abruptly, so that his words rang out almost like a report from a pistol, he asked:

"Why did you leave that incriminating piece of paper in my bed last night?"

His question was so unexpected that it took Gilda completely by surprise.

For a moment she stopped breathing. Then the colour swept up her face in a crimson tide which proclaimed her guilt without words.

Because she could think of nothing to refute his accusation, she bowed her head and was silent until the Marquis said:

"I am waiting for an answer to my question!"

"H-how did you . . . know it was I . . . who put it . . . there?" Gilda asked, and her voice was so low that it was almost impossible to hear what she said.

"My Valet saw you upstairs at a time when you were not in the Ball-Room," he replied, "and I cannot think of anybody else amongst my friends who would be involved in anything so reprehensible."

Gilda lowered her head even farther.

She felt that he was condemning her and after this would never speak to her again. She would have to go away, perhaps back home, but anyway into obscurity.

Then in a very different tone of voice the Marquis asked quietly:

"Will you tell me what happened?"

Gilda thought there was nothing else she could do but tell him the truth.

"Someone . . . a man . . ." she said a little incoherently, "when I was sitting in the . . . garden told me to . . . drop my . . . reticule."

"You obeyed him?"

"He told me twice in a whisper . . . and I do not know why . . . but I did as he said."

"Then what happened?"

"He picked it up and . . . gave it . . . back to me, and when I . . . thanked him he said it was . . . a pleasure and . . . walked away."

"Do you know who he was?"

"No . . . I had never . . . seen him . . . before."

There was a pause. Then the Marquis asked:

"Did you realise he had put something into your reticule?"

"Only a few minutes later . . . when I re-placed my . . . handkerchief in it."

"You were not expecting anything of this kind to happen?"

The question was sharp, as if, Gilda thought, he suspected that she was not telling the truth.

"No . . . of course . . . not!" she answered. "How could I . . . imagine anything like that would . . . occur at a . . . party given by . . . you?"

"Or at any other party, I should imagine," the Marquis added ironically.

"No . . . of course . . . not!"

"You swear to me," he said, "that you had no idea when this happened what this strange man had put inside your reticule?"

"None . . . whatever."

"What happened after that?"

Because she was frightened it took Gilda some time to relate that her dancing-partner had returned with a servant carrying lemonade for her and champagne for him.

As the music had started again they had walked back to the house.

"I felt there was something hard in my reticule," she said, "and I decided to go . . . upstairs and see what it was. Then in the . . . crowd I suddenly felt the ribbons on my arm tighten . . ."

It was difficult to go on, but after a moment she continued:

"I . . . I thought my bag was just being . . . caught by someone moving . . . beside me, until it . . . happened again. Then when I tried to hold . . . on to it with my right hand, I . . . touched a man's fingers!"

"What man?" the Marquis enquired.

"I do not . . . know."

"You saw him?"

"Yes . . . yes . . . I turned my head . . . he was tall with a high forehead . . . but I only had a quick . . . glimpse of him."

"Did he speak to you?"

For a moment Gilda could not remember. Then she answered:

"He said *'Pardon'* and . . . disappeared."

"Then what did you do?"

"I went upstairs to the . . . bedroom where I had left my . . . wrap when I arrived . . ."

"And opened your reticule!"

"Y-yes."

"What did you think when you looked inside?" the Marquis asked.

"For a moment . . . I did not . . . understand," Gilda said in a very low voice. "Then when I read about the . . . ships and the . . . movement of the troops, I was sure that what I was . . . carrying was . . . information that could be useful to the . . . enemy . . ."

Her voice died away as she said the last words, and she thought nothing could be more humiliating than to have to confess to the Marquis that she had been involved even inadvertently in enemy espionage.

"So you were perceptive enough to understand the importance of what had been placed in your reticule?" the Marquis asked.

She thought by the way he spoke that he was accusing her not only of being aware of the seriousness of what was written on the piece of paper but also of having been somehow instrumental in its being there.

"I swear to . . . you," she said, "I swear by . . . everything I hold . . . holy, that I have no . . . idea why this should . . . happen or what I was . . . supposed to do . . . about it."

Even as she spoke she knew that was untrue.

She was aware why she had been chosen and that it was because the spies or traitors, whatever they were, had thought her to be her sister.

With a sense of horror she remembered the jewel-case upstairs at the bottom of her wardrobe with its sovereigns at the bottom of it and the letter from the Bank saying how much money was deposited in Heloise's name.

It was Heloise's money — money she had obtained by betraying her own country — which might cost the lives of English soldiers and sailors, and even perhaps eventually English civilians like themselves.

Because the idea was so horrifying Gilda rose to her feet.

The Marquis looked at her face and saw it was deathly pale, and as she stood beside him she asked:

"What . . . could I do? How could I . . . explain to . . . anybody what had . . . occurred?"

"So you hid the incriminating papers in my

bed," he said slowly. "Why did you not give them to me?"

She looked away from him, knowing that she could not tell him the truthful answer to that question.

"I was afraid."

"Afraid of me, or afraid that you would be discovered with such papers in your possession and be brought to trial?"

His voice sounded hard and Gilda gave a little cry of sheer terror.

"Are you . . . saying that I shall be arrested?"

He did not answer and she gave a little sob and covered her face with her hands.

"I am . . . frightened . . . please . . . please . . . help me," she begged.

Then suddenly, as the Marquis did not reply, she looked up at him with the tears running down her face and asked:

"You are . . . not saying that I could be . . . hanged . . . or shot as a . . . s-spy?"

Because the idea was so terrifying and she thought the Marquis's expression was as grim as that of a Judge, she threw herself against him as she had done before and hid her face against his shoulder.

"S-save me . . . please . . . save me!" she sobbed. "It is not only that I am . . . afraid of . . . d-dying . . . but as Papa's daughter . . . how could I . . . disgrace him?"

Her words tumbled over one another, and as the Marquis felt her tremble against him convulsively as she had done before, he put his arm round her as if to support her.

In her misery Gilda just sobbed with her face against his shoulder, until after a little time he said very quietly:

"Stop crying! You came to me for protection, and I will protect you."

Gilda controlled her tears but she did not move away from him. She only held on to him as if comforted by the strength of his arm and the fact that she was close against his chest.

"C-can you . . . save . . . me?" she asked after a moment, her voice breaking on the words.

"I will save you," the Marquis said, "but I agree with you that it would be intolerable for your father's good name, which is venerated by those who served with him, to be dragged in the filth and shame which an enquiry would involve."

The relief of what he said made Gilda feel so weak that she thought she might fall to the ground.

Without being conscious of what she was doing, she moved even closer, as if only by doing so could she lose the terror which still left her trembling.

"But the only way I can help you," the Marquis said, "is if you tell me the whole and absolute truth."

He felt Gilda stiffen and went on:

"There is no other way by which I can sift the facts and extricate you from the position in which, perhaps through no fault of your own, you have become involved."

He thought that Gilda was very tense and after a moment he asked beguilingly:

"Will you not trust me?"

There was a pause before Gilda said:

"I . . . want to do so . . . but I . . . I am . . . afraid."

"Of me?"

"Of what you . . . might think."

There was a faint smile on the Marquis's lips which Gilda did not see as he asked:

"Does it matter to you what I think?"

"Of . . . course it . . . matters."

"Why?"

The question was sharp, and Gilda felt it was almost like an arrow piercing into the very depths of her being.

Now she was trembling again, but it was different from the way she had trembled before.

Unexpectedly the Marquis put his hand under her chin and turned her face up to his.

He looked down at her cheeks wet with tears, her lips quivering, and her blue eyes too shy to meet his.

It was impossible, he thought, for any woman to look more lovely or appealing, and he felt she was little more than a child.

"Tell me," he said, "why it matters to you what I think and feel about you."

She would have turned her face away again, but his fingers held her chin and made it impossible for her to do so.

She could only look up at him helplessly, thinking that he must see the love in her eyes and know that she was acutely conscious of his lips so near to hers.

"Tell me," the Marquis said again insistently, and it was a command.

Because she was so bemused, so frightened, and her will seemed to have snapped under the strain of his questioning, she told the truth.

"It is . . . because I . . . love you!" she said. "I . . . I know I have . . . no right to do so . . . but I cannot . . . help it."

"Just as I cannot help loving you," the Marquis said, and his lips came down on hers.

For a moment Gilda thought it could not be true and that she had died and was in Heaven.

Then the wonder of the Marquis's kiss and his lips on hers made her feel as if the darkness and fear were all left behind, and he carried her into the sunshine and up into the very heart of the sun.

It was so perfect, so rapturous, that she felt as if they were no longer two human people but one with the angels and with the music of a celestial choir singing all round them.

Then when she felt that no-one could feel such rapture, such joy, such wonder, and still live, the Marquis raised his head, and after an incoherent little sound Gilda said:

"I . . . love you! . . . I love you! I never knew . . . anyone could . . . be so . . . wonderful!"

Then, as if it was too much for her, she hid her face against him and felt the tears running once more down her cheeks.

The Marquis did not speak for a moment. Then he said in a voice that sounded strange:

"Tell me what you felt when I kissed you."

"How can I . . . express it in . . . words?" Gilda asked, and her voice held a rapturous note that no-one had ever heard before.

"I made you happy?" the Marquis said.

"I did not . . . know that a . . . kiss could be . . . like the sunshine . . . the flowers . . . a blessing from God . . ."

The Marquis, listening, knew that she was speaking her thoughts out loud.

"It is the first time you have been kissed?" he asked.

"How could . . . anyone . . . else make me feel . . . like that?" she asked.

The Marquis's arms tightened round her. Then he said:

"That is what I hoped it was, and since you love me, my beautiful one, how soon shall we be married?"

Gilda was very still.

Then, almost as if the glory of the sunshine he had given her with his lips vanished out of sight, she came back to clear, stark reality.

"Oh . . . no!" she said. "I . . . I cannot . . . marry . . . you!"

"Why not?"

Gilda thought wildly before she said:

"For one reason . . . you are too grand . . . too important to marry . . . somebody like . . . m-me."

"That is for me to decide," the Marquis said, "and since, as you are doubtless unaware, this is the first time I have ever asked anybody to marry me, I have no intention of being refused."

"B-but you . . . must be!" Gilda said quickly.

Now she raised her head from his shoulder.

"I . . . I cannot explain . . . I cannot tell you why . . . and it is the most . . . marvellous . . . glorious thing that ever happened to me that you should . . . ask me to be your . . . wife . . . but I have to . . . say 'no.' "

She moved away from him and walked towards the window almost as if she needed the air to go on breathing.

Having reached it, she held on to the window-sill, knowing that in refusing the Marquis she had closed the gates of Heaven against herself and never again would she know the glory and rapture he had given her with his kiss.

When he spoke she started because she had not realised he had followed her to the window and was just behind her.

"I asked you to trust me," he said quietly.

"I . . . do trust you, I would . . . trust you . . . with my . . . life!"

"Then what is the secret you are holding from me?"

Gilda drew in her breath and once again she was tense.

"W-what secret are you . . . talking about?"

"I want you to tell me that," the Marquis said.

Gilda clenched her hands together and tried desperately to think of how she could do what he asked.

As if he realised how difficult her decision was, the Marquis said:

"This morning I went to the War Office and looked up your father's record, a very distinguished record of which any country would be proud."

"I wish Papa . . . could hear you . . . say that," Gilda whispered.

"The records also told me," the Marquis went on, "that your mother is dead and that your father left two daughters."

As he spoke Gilda felt as if the ceiling had suddenly crashed onto her head and the whole room was dark.

She could not speak, for her voice was constricted in her throat. Then the Marquis asked:

"What has happened to Heloise? For I am quite certain that you are Gilda!"

There was a terrifying silence until Gilda asked:

"H-how did you . . . guess?"

He smiled.

"Because you are very different from your sister. Ever since you returned to London after running away from my dinner-party, you have puzzled, intrigued, and surprised me, and I could not understand why you had changed."

Gilda bent her head.

"Heloise . . . died! She came . . . home to . . . stay, and died of an . . . overdose of laudanum . . . so I took her . . . place."

"Why?"

"Because I had . . . no money . . . and if I had . . . stayed on as Heloise told me to . . . do, I would have . . . starved."

As she spoke she thought it sounded a feeble, unconvincing excuse, and it seemed when she spoke of it a very reprehensible way to behave.

The Marquis, however, did not speak, and after a moment she said:

"Now you . . . know why you cannot . . . marry somebody who . . . lied to you . . . and deceived Lady Neyland . . . after she had been so . . . kind to . . . Heloise."

"Heloise was not as kind to her as you have been."

"That is . . . partly because I . . . felt I had to make . . . reparation for my . . . sins."

"I do not think that your sister would have thought of it in quite that way," the Marquis said drily.

"But it was wrong . . . very wrong," Gilda said. "Please . . . please . . . forgive me . . . and let me go home . . . I will never . . . trouble you . . . again."

"To starve?" he enquired.

"I . . . I will manage . . . somehow."

"And you will do that without having any regrets or heart-burnings of what you are giving up?"

Gilda thought wryly of how truly heart-burning it would be to leave him and never see him again.

But regrets were something different.

Aloud she said:

"I will never . . . regret the time I . . . have been here in . . . London . . . and meeting . . . you."

"Does that matter so much?"

"Of course it . . . does. I did not know that . . . anyone like you . . . existed, and when Heloise . . . talked about you I . . . thought I . . . hated you."

"You hated me?" the Marquis echoed in surprise.

"I was sure, from what Heloise . . . said, that you had no . . . intention of . . . marrying her, and I thought it was . . . cruel to raise her hopes and prevent her from . . . marrying anybody . . . else."

"Like Sir Humphrey Grange?"

"He is . . . horrible!" Gilda said. "But there . . . must have been . . . other men."

"Not in the same position as I am."

"Your position is . . . unimportant."

"Do you believe that?"

"Of course I believe it! If I were going to . . .

marry somebody, it would be . . . because he was . . . a man I loved. Whether he was . . . rich or poor, important or a nobody, is of no real . . . significance."

The thoughts Gilda had had about this before seemed to tumble from her lips without her really considering what she was saying.

Then she turned her back on the Marquis to stare out the window with unseeing eyes before she asked:

"Now that you . . . know the truth . . . what do you want me . . . to do?"

As she spoke she could see the vegetable-patch at home on which she must plant the food she must grow to live on, the rooms inside the house quiet and empty, and if she was afraid or lonely there would be no-one to protect her.

Then the Marquis put his hands on her shoulders and turned her round to face him.

"Shall I tell you what I want you to do?" he asked.

There was an expression in his eyes and a note in his voice which made Gilda feel that once again she was dazzled by a radiant light that came not from the sky but from him.

He did not wait for her answer, but said:

"We are going to be married immediately, my lovely one, and there will be no spies to frighten you, no secrets that you dare not reveal, no starvation or loneliness, only me. Is that what you want?"

"B-but you . . . cannot . . . you . . . must not
. . ." Gilda began.

The Marquis pulled her close against him,
and his lips stopped her from saying any more.

Only when he had given her the sun, the
moon, and the stars and she was no longer
alone but a part of him did they both come
back to earth.

"How can you make me feel like this?" the
Marquis asked. "I never thought it was possible
that I could love anybody as I love you."

"It . . . it cannot be . . . true!"

He smiled.

"It will take me a long time to prove it, but
first, my darling, before we plan our wedding I
must solve Lord Hawkesbury's problem and
see that the spies of Napoleon Bonaparte are
behind bars."

"How can you do that?" Gilda asked.

The Marquis looked down at her face radiant
with an expression he had never seen on any
other woman's face.

He knew that her love came not only from
her heart but from her soul and had something
spiritual about it, very different from anything
he had known before.

Then because it was impossible when he was
touching her to think of anything else, he
moved to the mantelpiece to stand with his
back to it.

"Now let me consider what you have told
me," he said.

"I have . . . not told you . . . everything."

"No?"

"I am . . . ashamed . . . so desperately ashamed . . . but you must . . . know."

"Know what?"

Not looking at him, because she felt so humiliated, Gilda told him the secrets of her sister's jewel-case and the money that was in Coutts Bank.

The Marquis's lips tightened in a straight line, and when she had finished speaking Gilda stood looking at him before she said in a broken little voice:

"Perhaps now . . . you will . . . cease to . . . love me."

The Marquis smiled and held out his arms and she ran towards him like a homing-pigeon.

"I shall have to teach you about love, my precious one," he said. "The real love that you and I have for each other can survive anything, however abominable."

"If you had committed a thousand murders I would still love you!" Gilda said passionately.

The Marquis did not kiss her but put his cheek against hers and said:

"Now we have to think very seriously of everything that could give us a clue, not to the first man who put the information into your reticule, because I know who he is."

"You do?"

"Yes, he works in the Foreign Office," the Marquis replied. "But it is the recipient of this treachery who matters. Describe him once again."

"I . . . I did not get a close look at him," Gilda said with a sigh. "I just turned my head as he said *'Pardon.'* "

The Marquis gave an exclamation.

"As he said — what?"

" *'Pardon'!*" Gilda repeated.

"You are quite certain he said it in French rather than English?"

"I never thought of it before," Gilda replied, "but that is what he said."

"Then I know who he is!"

"You do?"

The Marquis nodded.

"There was only one foreigner at the party last night — the man who accompanied the Princess de Lieven because the Ambassador was otherwise engaged. He is a Russian! Now we know who our enemy is!"

"I am glad . . . so very . . . very glad!" Gilda exclaimed.

"So am I," the Marquis agreed, "for now we can think only about ourselves and our future."

He put both his arms round her and pulled her closer to him and said:

"Where do you want to live after we are married?"

"With you!"

The Marquis laughed.

"You may be sure of that, but I was thinking that as you are a country girl you would doubtless be happier in the country than in London."

"To be with you in the country would be the most . . . marvellous thing that could . . . happen to me."

"Then that is where we will be," he promised.

He would have kissed her, but for the moment she resisted.

"There is . . . something I want to . . . ask you."

"What is it?"

"Are you quite . . . quite certain it is really . . . me you want as your wife? I am very . . . unsophisticated and . . . ignorant of your life . . . and the Social World in which you . . . live."

She paused before she went on:

"Supposing when you marry me you find I am only a . . . pale reflection of Heloise . . . and you would have been . . . happier with her?"

Once again the Marquis turned Gilda's face up to his.

"Listen to me," he said, "and it is important that you should know the truth."

"I am . . . listening."

"I would never have married your sister because, although when I first saw her I thought she was the most beautiful person I had ever seen, I soon knew that her beauty was only superficial, and beneath such loveliness she was selfish, avaricious, and, as we both know, treacherous!"

The Marquis paused for a moment, thinking how his instinct was never wrong and he had sensed this about Heloise even though if he had said it aloud nobody would have believed him.

"What I feel about you, my dearest dear, is very different," he went on. "Your face is as beautiful as the flowers and your hair is like the sunshine. What you give me when you speak of your love is divine so that I know it comes from your soul."

Gilda gave a little cry of sheer happiness and the Marquis said:

"That is why we will not speak of the past again. You must forget your sister and make sure that everybody else forgets her too. You are not a reflection of her. She was just a pale, distorted reflection of you."

"You really . . . believe that is . . . true?"

"We will always tell each other the truth," the Marquis said, "and the truth is, my lovely Gilda, that all my life I have looked deep into women's hearts, hoping to find real love, but I never found it until I met you."

Gilda gave a little exclamation of delight and put her arm round his neck to pull his head down to hers.

"Are you . . . sure?"

"Very, very sure."

Her lips were very close to his as she whispered:

"Teach me how not to . . . disappoint you. Teach me how to be . . . everything you want me to be. I have nothing to give you . . . except my love . . . and that is . . . all of me."

"That is all I want," the Marquis said.

Then he was kissing her until once again he carried her up into the Heavens and they found a love which was so perfect that it came not only from their hearts and souls but from God.

# About the Author

Barbara Cartland, the world's most famous romantic novelist, who is also an historian, playwright, lecturer, political speaker and television personality, has now written over 300 books.

She has also had many historical works published and has written four autobiographies as well as the biographies of her mother and that of her brother Ronald Cartland, who was the first Member of Parliament to be killed in W.W.II. This book has a preface by Sir Winston Churchill and has just been republished with an introduction by Sir Arthur Bryant.

Barbara Cartland has sold 200 million books over the world, more than half of these in the U.S.A. She broke the world record in 1975 by writing twenty-three books and the four subsequent years with 20, 21, 23 and 24. In addition her album of love songs has just been published, sung with the Royal Philharmonic Orchestra.

Barbara Cartland, who is a Dame of the Order of St. John of Jerusalem has championed the cause for old people and founded the first Romany Gypsy Camp in the world.

Barbara Cartland is deeply interested in Vitamin Therapy and is President of the British National Association for Health. Her book the *Magic of Honey* has sold in millions all over the world.

She has a magazine *The World of Romance* and her Barbara Cartland Romantic World Tours will, in conjunction with British Airways, carry travelers to England, Egypt, India, France, Germany and Turkey.